The Fai

on

Pineapple Island

Joy Wodhams

Copyright © 2015

Joy Wodhams

The Family

on

Pineapple Island

Thank you for ordering this book. If you enjoy it you may like to try others by Joy Wodhams

FICTION FOR ADULTS
Affair With An Angel
The Reluctant Bride
Never Sleep With A Neighbour!

CHILDREN'S FICTION
The Mystery of Craven Manor
A Lion In My Bed

SHORT STORY COLLECTIONS
The Floater
The Girl at Table Nine

Joy Wodhams has been writing as long as she can remember. She is the descendant of five generations of theatre and circus gymnasts, trapeze artists, singers, musicians and songwriters. As far as she is aware she is the first fiction writer in the family and is also an artist and tutor.

The Family on Pineapple Island is her eighth novel, a heart warming and humorous story that can be enjoyed not only by children aged 9 to 12 but by their parents and grandparents also.

1

Eggs, More Eggs and Philomena Haggerty

Before each of the Colonel's visits to Pineapple Island Fred Scarrot would make his family stop whatever they were doing and form up for inspection: clean hands, tidy hair, proper clothing – he didn't want the Colonel seeing Poppy in that awful red dress that made her look forty instead of fifteen, or Jack in his rock star jacket with those shiny things all over it.

Afterwards he would line them up on the jetty, largest to smallest. Himself at the head, followed by his wife Alice; next Jack, then Poppy who was a year older than Jack but small and plump; then eight year old Jenny, and finally Tommy, the youngest.

Today they formed a reluctant, fidgety line as they watched the Colonel's boat chugging towards them. Jenny was the only one who waited patiently and without complaint. She rather enjoyed her little chats with the stern old Colonel, who was not really stern at all, and the chocolate fudge that he always carried with him was the best in Cumbria. But even she felt that it was all a bit unnecessary. After all, the Colonel didn't come just once or twice a year. He came every other Saturday.'Here he is,' said Mr Scarrot. 'Now, do stop that!' he called to Tommy, who on the end of the line was heaving heavy sighs of boredom. 'And Alice, pull your tummy in!'

Mrs Scarrot glared at him indignantly but did as he ordered.

And then the Colonel had landed and he and Mr Scarrot were grinning at each other and pumping each other's hands up and down as if they had not met for years. Poppy was sure she even saw a tear in the Colonel's faded blue eyes. When he took out a handkerchief and trumpeted into it, she was sure.

Once the Colonel had shared out his bag of fudge, asked after Mrs Scarrot's health, admired Poppy's nice rosy cheeks and chucked Jenny and Tommy beneath their chins, they were allowed to go. Only Jenny lingered, curious to know what was inside the large wooden crate that the Colonel had brought across with him. There were air holes in the lid.

Mrs Scarrot and Poppy returned to the hen house. Mrs Scarrot opened a new sack of mash and began to fill the feeders.

'They've been going on like that ever since the war,' she said, 'and Fred still won't tell me what it's all about.'

Poppy glanced up with surprise from the chicken she had been inspecting. It had been pecked by the others and had lost its tail feathers. 'You mean you don't know?'

'Of course I don't know!' Mrs Scarrot's voice rose sharply. 'Every year I've asked your Dad and he just touches his nose and smiles. I even asked the Colonel himself once but he wouldn't tell me either. I wouldn't be surprised if they haven't forgotten themselves what started it all!' She shook out the last of the mash and rolled up the empty sack. 'All I know is that your Dad performed some special service for the Colonel when he served under him and the Colonel was grateful. Then when your Dad lost his job at the car factory, when you and Jack were just toddlers, the Colonel said we could

come and live on his island. Not that I'm not pleased a.
it does drive me wild, not knowing the whys and w.
things.'

'Well, you don't give people islands for nothing,' said I __ ᴊ. ᴊne
set down the pecked chicken in the run and glared a warning at the
others. 'I reckon Dad must have saved his life at least.' A dreamy look
came over her round rosy face. 'I can just imagine it. The Colonel
lying on the ground, unconscious, blood trickling from a huge gash in
his skull. And Dad unsheathing his sword and defending him against
a wild savage horde. I think it's terribly romantic.'

She gazed at the square stocky figure of her father, who was
waving goodbye to the Colonel, and tried to visualise the dashing
heroic figure he must have been in those far off days.

'I don't think your Dad ever had a sword. And I'm sure there
weren't any wild savage hordes in Wiltshire where he was stationed.
Might be now, of course, with all these rock and rollers.' Mrs Scarrot
rose, shook out her skirt and picked up the bowl of eggs collected
from the nesting boxes. 'Anyway, we're never going to find out.'

'What's for lunch?' asked Tommy as she carried the eggs into the
kitchen. He was sitting at the wooden table pasting pictures of
football players into his scrapbook.

'Spanish omelette.'

'Is that eggs?'

'Afraid so. The hens won't stop laying and we have to use them
up.'

Tommy's five year old treble deepened with disgust. 'We have
nothing to eat but eggs and strawberries lately!'

'Now, Tommy, you know that's not true. Besides, you should
count your blessings. Some children never have strawberries. And
put that stuff away, you know you're not supposed to have glue on
the table.'

'They're lucky,' Tommy said bitterly, ignoring her scolding.

'You'd be the first to complain if Dad had sold them all to the
shops. And you've always said they're your favourite fruit.'

'Only when there's just a few. Not when there's lots and lots forever!'

'Never mind. In a few days they'll all be picked.'

'Bobby's mother doesn't make him eat eggs and strawberries every day,' Tommy mumbled as he closed his scrapbook and furtively picked up the scales of glue that were stuck to the table. 'Bobby Peabody has frozen He-Man Hamburgers and Dream Surprise and Tasty Chicken Morsels in Golden Batter.'

'And spots too, I shouldn't wonder. Anyway, we're having real hamburgers for dinner tonight. Home made.'

Tommy brightened. 'With chips?'

Mrs Scarrot laughed. 'With chips,' she promised. She picked up the first egg and cracked it on the edge of her brown mixing bowl. 'Now why don't you go and help Dad while I make lunch?'

Tommy's small shoulders slumped with fatigue. 'I've been awfully busy this morning. I'm quite worn out. Why can't the others help?'

'Poppy's digging over the chicken run, Jack's weeding the onion beds and Jenny's hanging out my washing,' Mrs Scarrot returned patiently. 'Anyway, I thought you'd want to see the new rabbits the Colonel brought.'

'Rabbits! Why didn't you say so?' Tiredness forgotten, Tommy shot from the kitchen like a bullet from a gun, leaving his mother with a rueful grin to rescue the overturned bottle of glue.

But hurry as he might, Jenny was, of course, there before him, crouched over the open crate with soft mews of pleasure. Her spectacles had fallen down to the tip of her nose. She peered over their rims at the crate's moving contents.

'Let me see, let me see!' yelled Tommy, throwing himself down beside her.

'Sssh, you'll frighten them. They're all bewildered already.'

'Gar! Aren't they *big*? They're as big as - as big as houses!'

"New Zealand Whites,' said Mr Scarrot. 'Meat rabbits.'

'Meat?' echoed Jenny. She pushed her spectacles back to the

bridge of her nose and stared at her father with dawning horror. 'You mean - you mean they're going to be killed? For eating?'

'Not them. These are for breeding, but their offspring will go to the butcher in Keswick.'

'But that's awful.'

Tommy's lip jutted. 'I thought they were to be pets. For Jenny and me.'

Mr Scarrot shook his head. 'Sorry, Tommy, not these. But you will have a pet one day, I promise. A proper pet.'

Tommy aimed a half hearted kick at the crate. 'Stupid things anyway,' he muttered. 'They don't *do* anything.'

They left Mr Scarrot pondering on his next project. A cow? Two, maybe. But how to get them to the island? Even if you could persuade them into the boat, the silly things would probably step off halfway across the lake

'I'm going to see Philomena Haggerty,' said Jenny, her voice still small. Tommy followed as she walked with slow steps towards the hen house.

Poppy had just finished the chicken run and everything was neat and tidy. 'Wipe your feet before you go in,' she joked.

Slipping inside the wire door and closing it behind her, Jenny moved unerringly towards the third chicken from the right in the far corner. Tommy watched for a while but soon began to fidget. Watching someone else in silent communion with a chicken was pretty boring.

'How d'you know that's her?' he asked at last. 'Out of two dozen?'

'She comes to me,' said Jenny, her eyes still locked with the chicken's.

'It could be one of the others pretending to be her.'

'Don't be daft. Anyway, Philomena's different. Look at her eyes, they're all nice and soft. And her smile. Her beak goes up just a bit at one side, see? Sort of wistful. She's lovely.'

Tommy could still see no difference between Philomena and the other twenty three Rhode Island Red chickens, try as he might.

'Aw,' he said, losing patience. 'I'm going to see if lunch is ready.'

Halfway up the path to the house he remembered what lunch was. Eggs. Again. His face lengthened. Life was boring. Boring food. Boring rabbits. Boring chickens. And having to do chores, that was boring, too. Really, he couldn't think of a thing that wasn't boring. He'd be glad when he started school.

'I've made chocolate brownie pudding for afters,' said his mother as he entered the kitchen.

Chocolate brownie pudding! You couldn't call *that* boring. His face shortened again.

2

Extensions, Pianos And A Raft

If there was one thing Mr Scarrot enjoyed more than any other, more even than growing vegetables, it was building extensions. Nothing could surpass the pleasure of sawing wood, banging in nails and putting on roofs. The tiny two-roomed house that had been their home when he and Mrs Scarrot first came to the island had not dismayed him one jot. The very next day he had set about building his first extension and now, thirteen years later, there were more extensions than original house.

Altogether there were ten rooms. They followed no particular plan. To get from Jenny's bedroom to the bathroom, for instance, you had to pass through the dining room, while a trip from the sitting room to the kitchen included a brief visit to the washhouse. But no one minded. The house stood up, it was warm and snug, and the rain only came in when the wind blew from the east. In fact the rest of the family thought Mr Scarrot was pretty clever to have built it.

One fine summer day Mr and Mrs Scarrot were painting the outside of his latest extension - another sitting room, twice as big as the old one. Mrs Scarrot's face as she slapped paint on the end wall was thoughtful.

'I do wish we had a piano,' she said suddenly. 'Now we've got a bigger room there'd be space for one.'

Mr Scarrot loaded his brush with Festive Pink gloss and worked it into the panels of the door. It was a nice colour. Cheerful. Much better than that Rose Pompadour they'd used for Tommy's bedroom.

'What on earth would we do with a piano?' he asked.

The Festive Pink and the Bermuda Blue of the kitchen were his favourites, he decided, although the green on Jack's room was nice. Pity he didn't know its name, but he'd bought the tin cheap without a label and until it was opened he hadn't known whether it would be red, green or striped purple. Anyway, which colours you liked wasn't important. What mattered was which colours were on Special Offer in the hardware shop. Or better still, Discontinued. You got them for half price if they were discontinued. Of course, some people might think it a bit odd having the outside of a house all different colours but *he* liked it. Made it look like a posy of garden flowers, he thought. Besides being cheaper.

'I'd play it,' said Mrs Scarrot.

'Play what?' Mr Scarrot paused, his brush dripping paint on to the toe of his right boot. 'You never told me you could play the piano!'

'You never asked. As a matter of fact,' Mrs Scarrot said proudly, 'I've still got my Sixth Grade certificate in the back of my writing case.'

'Well, blow me down.' Mr Scarrot gazed at her in wonder, thinking that she could still surprise him after going on for twenty years. He did admire people who had a talent, though. Especially when they had a certificate to prove it.

He tried to open the new door so that he could paint the edges but it was jammed. That was not unusual. Mr Scarrot's doors frequently had to be kicked open and shoved shut. It was because he scorned the use of a spirit level, believing that he had been born with a natural eye for verticals and horizontals.

'Shan't be a minute.' Climbing through the open window he counted three and hurled himself at the door from the inside, turning with practised ease in mid-rush to slam the sole of his boot against the left hand panel.

'How would we get it to the island?' asked Mrs Scarrot as he tumbled through the opening. 'If we bought one, I mean?'

He picked up his brush and thought. It would be a problem, all right. You couldn't load a dirty great piano into an old rowing boat that was built for no more than five people, and small ones at that. You'd be lucky if you got ten yards out from the shore without sinking. No, something else was needed. Something that would take the weight. And the size. He returned his brush to the can of Festive Pink paint and sat down on a nearby tree stump. He thought better sitting down.

Half an hour later he had made his decision. He would build a raft.

'Don't know why I didn't think of it before,' he told Mrs Scarrot jubilantly. 'It'll solve more problems than just a piano!'

Once Mr Scarrot had an idea he had to begin immediately. The thought of waiting until tomorrow was unbearable. All the same, he felt a bit mean leaving poor old Alice with two walls and a window frame still to paint. Pity the older children were not at home. But perhaps ...

He found Jenny on her knees in her bedroom, surrounded by the past week's copies of the Daily Sun.

'What are you doing?'

'They've printed a different cartoon every day but the captions are all mixed up. You have to sort them out and put them against the right ones.'

'What's the prize?'

'A dishwasher.'

'Oh.' Mr Scarrot lost interest. 'Jenny, love, how'd you like to help your mother outside?'

'Help her to do what?' asked Jenny warily.

'Paint the extension.'

'Paint ...' The beginnings of incredulous delight lit up Jenny's face. 'But you've never allowed me to paint before.'

'And I wouldn't now if it weren't an emergency. So don't let me down, will you?'

Jenny's small jaw firmed and her eyes widened. 'No, Dad. No, I won't. Truly I won't.'

Travelling the countryside with his van full of vegetables for sale, Mr Scarrot had got to know all the traders, farmers and businessmen in the area. He had long formed the habit of jotting down in a dog-eared red notebook the sources of any materials that might help him in his building, so when he set out to buy twenty empty oil drums he knew exactly where to locate them.

Their owner knew how to drive a hard bargain, but so did Mr Scarrot. An hour later he returned to Lake Kenmere with the last of the drums, having left behind eight pound notes and a sack of cabbages that were a bit on the limp side.

Three sacks of potatoes, two nets of onions and a box of carrots later he had the timber, the rope and the nails.

Even with Jack's help it took two full days of sawing and planing, hammering and lashing, but by sunset on the evening of the second day, when the sun was casting a soft rosy glow over the calm water, the raft was finished. Eighteen foot long, ten foot wide. The corners might not be perfectly square but it bobbed and bounced as proudly as the Kon-Tiki against the sandy bank of the lake.

The Scarrot family raised a loud cheer and Mr Scarrot bowed gallantly and offered his arm with a flourish to his wife. Then Jack placed four garden chairs on the raft, and while he and Mr Scarrot punted, Mrs Scarrot, the two girls and Tommy sat in state and were carried with great majesty round and round the island on the raft's maiden voyage.

A week later they found the piano of Mrs Scarrot's dreams. It belonged to Mrs Freda Perkins, a bony bustling lady who kept a guest house in Keswick and had a low opinion of objects that took up space without earning their keep. She could seat another two paying guests in her lounge with that old thing gone, she told the Scarrots. Mr Scarrot agreed but he felt sorry for the guests. The tall narrow room with its mottled carpet that wouldn't show the dirt and the rows of wooden chairs around the walls was more like a dentist's waiting room than a holiday 'home from home'.

But the piano was beautiful, an Edwardian upright of gleaming rosewood inlaid with a pattern of lilies and leaves. It had a silver candle sconce at each end, and Mrs Scarrot was entranced.

They would have taken the piano away immediately but it was far too heavy. Curbing their impatience, they waited until Mrs Perkins' lodgers began to drift down from their bedrooms and at last, after Mrs Perkins had pounced on two stalwart lads from Liverpool and a brawny butcher from St. Helens to help, the piano was manhandled down the steps of the guest house and into the waiting van, which gave a protesting wheeze and sank four inches on its springs.

'We'll have to drive back slowly,' said Mr Scarrot. 'I think we'd better have lunch in Keswick before we start.'

They found a shiny little side-street café with chrome and red Formica tables and those hard plastic chairs that have a round hole cut out of the back to allow people's bottoms to poke through. It was not the sort of place that Mr Scarrot would have chosen, being the first time he had taken Mrs Scarrot out for lunch in ten years, but the parking space outside decided him.

The steak and kidney pie came in a silver foil container, accompanied by a small cluster of pale chips and a spoonful of emerald green peas. He bit into the pie critically.

'Not like yours, love,' he said, gazing with a warm glow of happiness at his wife, who was not only plump and beautiful but could cook like an angel.

It was a good day, he decided, and when he saw Mrs Scarrot dreaming in front of the glamorous photographs in the window of a ladies' hair salon he urged her in a rush of reckless generosity to go inside.

Later on, as he eased the heavy van down the narrow country lanes towards Lake Kenmere, he stole glances at her. She looked absolutely lovely, he thought, all soft and pink and smiling, just like the day they were married, with her hair in a coronet of glossy brown curls on the top of her head.

An irresistible impulse overcame him and, bringing the van to a halt, he turned and gave his wife a big smacking kiss, just to show how much he loved her.

Perhaps it had been a mistake to stop the van, he thought half an hour later as he struggled to get it started again, but Alice's surprised pleasure had been worth it.

When at last they reached Kenmere Mr Scarrot called on the Colonel's gardener and gamekeeper to help him lift the piano out of the van and on to the raft.

'Blimey, it's heavy!' Jim Firbank gasped as they struggled to centre the piano's great weight on the raft. 'Come on, Hector, we'd better go across and help them unload it.'

The raft was halfway to the island when Mrs Scarrot felt something tickle her toes and saw with horror that water was lapping over the edge of the planks.

'We're sinking! Oh, my piano!' she wailed. 'My lovely piano! And my *hair*!'

Mr Scarrot stared in disbelief at the water which was now creeping towards the shining rosewood feet of the piano. Surely twenty oil drums were enough to keep anything afloat? He gulped. 'Everybody off! Quick, over the side, we'll have to hold the raft up and swim with it to the island.'

Without further hesitation he leapt into the water, followed by Jim Firbank and Hector Peabody. Mrs Scarrot dithered, clutching at her coronet of curls.

'Come on, Alice!' Reluctantly she jumped.

Without their combined weight the raft rose in the water and slowly, sluggishly, they inched it towards the island.

Once Jim Firbank had won a medal for life saving. 'But I never had to life save a piano before,' he gasped as he tried to remember his side-stroke.

Years, mourned Mrs Scarrot. Years since I last had a hairdo and now it's all ruined.

Hector Peabody snorted as water rushed up his nostrils and he remembered too late that his pockets were full of shotgun cartridges.

Mr Scarrot urged them on.

'Go to it, lads,' he shouted, spitting out a surprised Water Boatman that had not looked where it was going. 'Alice, stop worrying about your hair and push!'

'It's all very well for you,' she gasped. 'You've hardly any hair to worry about!'

On the shore the Scarrot children watched anxiously.

'They're all going to drown,' wailed Jenny.

'Don't be silly,' snapped Poppy. 'Mam's not going to lose her piano now.'

D'you think I should go out and help?' asked Jack, whose method of swimming, an unorthodox butterfly stroke, drenched all within range.

'You'd do more harm than good. At least the piano's still dry. You'd be more useful if you fetched some dry towels for when they land.'

'You fetch them,' Jack responded huffily.

'All right, I will. *You* can make some cocoa. They'll need a hot drink when they get out, you know how cold that water is out in the middle.'

Later, when it was all over, when the piano had been landed and Mr Scarrot had rowed the men back to land, the family gathered in the sitting room.

'You've still got a bit of bulrush in your hair,' said Mr Scarrot and plucked it from his wife's bedraggled locks. 'I'm sorry about your hairdo, love.'

Mrs Scarrot glanced into the mirror over the fireplace, then turned to look at her beautiful piano, glowing like rose-brown satin in the mellow light of an oil lamp. Lifting the lid, she softly played a single note and they listened in silence to the pure silvery sound.

'Never mind, Fred,' she said softly. 'What's a hairdo, compared with that?'

3

The Toy Soldiers

Looking back, Mr Scarrot wondered how he had ever managed without the raft. It was all so easy now. He could transport anything he wanted from the mainland to the island: building materials, furniture - why, there was no limit to what he could carry (once he had lashed a few extra oil drums to the raft). He might even look for the brass bedstead that Mrs Scarrot had wanted for so long.

It was with this intention that Mr Scarrot attended his first auction. He had noticed the placard outside The Gamekeeper pub when he was delivering a box of onions to Mrs Crabbe's shop next door and had made a note to go back there the following Tuesday, when Messrs Hardin, Frinton & Knowle would be auctioning the cottage that had belonged to old Mr Cartwright and all its contents.

When he returned on Tuesday, the auction had already started and a hubbub of noise came from within. Mr Scarrot almost turned tail but then he decided he might as well find out what it was all about. If they didn't have a brass bedstead he would come straight out again.

Two and a half hours later he emerged, the proud owner of not only a large brass bedstead but also six brass candlesticks, an Edward the Seventh coronation chamber pot, a cast iron frying pan and a

1930s lawnmower.

After that Mr Scarrot was hooked. Whenever an auction was advertised and he had some spare money in his pocket he was sure to be there. Soon the sight of the raft returning across the lake after a sale was the signal for all the Scarrot family to drop whatever they were doing and run down to the jetty, agog to see what Dad had bought this time.

His purchases were often interesting and always unpredictable. Once he brought home a complete library of old books, boxes and boxes of them, that sent out a sweet mildewy smell when they were opened. Another time, an Indian elephant's foot and a moth-eaten stag's head that came from Major Pointer's old home. Jenny decorated the foot with strings of beads and scarlet paint on its toenails, and the head was hung on Tommy's bedroom door for hoop-la. Once there was a huge brass gong that the auctioneer said was from Tibet. When it was struck, the sound echoed for a full ten minutes, nails fell out of the woodwork and waves rippled all the way across the lake.

In no time at all the rooms filled up with furniture and ornaments, and the children could no longer tear through the house like Mongol hordes through ancient China but had to pick their way through ever narrowing passages as more and more auction 'bargains' were squeezed into the house.

A day came when Mrs Scarrot found her route to the kitchen barred by three tables, one of marble and two with holes in the middle for plant pots.

'Do you know,' she said later to Poppy, 'do you know that we now have twenty two tables?'

Poppy stared at her and went away.

'You're wrong,' she said when she returned. 'There are twenty four!'

Two days later there were twenty seven. For of all the things that were sold at auction, tables held a special fascination for Mr Scarrot. He collected every kind imaginable. Tables of brass and gilt, wood and papier maché. Tables inlaid with mother of pearl, sycamore and yew. Or decorated with wavy haired ladies, Greek borders and cabbage roses. Regency tables, Queen Anne tables, painted and polished tables, tables with varnish so sticky that your fingers stuck to it. In short, every table that was offered. If it had four legs and was flat on top, Mr Scarrot bid for it.

In between tables he bought other things. Nine chests with pull-out flaps, secret drawers or hidden panels, four wardrobes, a tallboy, two sofas and an ottoman with a leopard skin top. A mirror draped with faded gilt cherubs for Poppy, an old ticking metronome for Jack, a Swiss music box that played Brahms' Lullaby for Jenny and a stuffed owl in a glass case for Tommy. For Charlie, who was not yet born but was expected very shortly) there was a Victorian ivory rattle, and Mrs Scarrot, whose hairdo had been ruined during the journey with the piano, received a silver backed brush and comb.

One evening Mr Scarrot announced that a sale was to take place the following day at a big country house near Keswick.

'Perhaps the children would like to come,' he said.

They stared at each other with delight.

'Well, I don't mind,' said Mrs Scarrot, 'as long as nobody else gets bitten by the auction bug. It's bad enough one person filling the house with junk every week, we don't want more!'

'An auction,' Jenny whispered when she slipped outside to tell Philomena Haggerty the news. 'We're going to an auction!'

'Now remember,' Mr Scarrot warned next morning as they tiptoed through the front door into the huge marble floored hall of the country house, 'Don't rub your noses or scratch your heads or you might find you've bought something you don't want!'

All the items for sale had a label pasted or tied to them, and on each label was a number.

'That's the lot number,' Mr Scarrot explained. 'The auctioneer starts with Lot Number One and goes through all the numbers in order until he reaches the end.'

The sale was not due to start for another half hour. The Scarrots wandered up and down amongst the crowds, examining the items to be sold.

'Where's Tommy?' Mrs Scarrot asked. The crowds were dense now and there was no sign of him. 'I hope he hasn't gone outside.'

'There he is.' said Poppy, catching a glimpse of his bright green jersey through a gap in the crowd.

Tommy's nose was pressed flat against the glass front of a large showcase and his eyes were dark blue with longing.

'Look, Dad,' he said to Mr Scarrot. His voice was almost a whisper.

In the case were hundreds of tiny lead soldiers. They were very old and their blue and scarlet uniforms and plumed helmets were finely detailed. With them were prancing horses and cannons and they were all so real that you could almost hear the tramping feet and the booming guns and the whinnying of the horses.

'Will you buy them for me, Dad?'

Mr Scarrot patted Tommy's head and smiled sadly. He knew that the toy soldiers would fetch a very high price. 'I'm sorry, Tommy. They'll be much too expensive.'

Tommy said nothing but as they moved away to find a space near the front of the crowd, his fingers counted the coins in his pockets. He had three weeks pocket money. Surely it would be enough.

The toy soldiers were Lot 43. Tommy had no interest in anything that came before but the others watched as the porters held up the items in turn.

At first the children wondered how the auctioneer was getting his bids for no one spoke except the auctioneer himself. He kept up a constant stream of talk. 'Who'll give me ten?' he asked. 'Ten I'm offered - fifteen - twenty five in the corner - twenty five - who'll give me thirty? -thirty five - going at thirty five - going for the first time - going for the second time - SOLD!' (with a loud bang of his hammer).

Then Poppy remembered Mr Scarrot's warning. She glanced around and saw with interest that people *were* bidding, and all in different ways. One man tapped his teeth with a pen, another tugged his right ear, a third waved his rolled up newspaper and a fourth winked his left eye. Poppy thought the auctioneer was very clever to see all the bids. She saw that his eyes were moving constantly up and down and across the room.

It was another half an hour before they reached Lot 43. 'A very fine and complete collection of 19th century model soldiers, a total of four hundred, together with horses and cannon.'

Poppy felt Tommy stiffen beside her, and in the moment's hush before the bidding started, his small clear voice piped out:

'One and sixpence!'

There was a stunned silence until from a corner of the room came a tiny snort of laughter. It was followed by a chuckle from someone else, and soon the whole roomful of people was laughing, some holding their sides as they let out great guffaws. Tommy's face paled and then it flushed a deep pink and tears started to his eyes. Poppy rounded on the crowd.

'Stop it!' she yelled. 'Stop it! What are you laughing at?'

A little shamefaced now, the crowd quietened and there was much shuffling of feet and clearing of throats.

The auctioneer bent from his rostrum and spoke to Tommy kindly. 'I'm sorry, young man. But you see, these are not ordinary toy soldiers.' He straightened and his voice resumed its former brisknness. 'Now, who will start the bidding at a hundred?'

A *hundred?* 'Does he mean a hundred pennies?' asked Tommy, bewildered.

Poppy swallowed. 'I think he means a hundred pounds.' Now she understood why people had laughed.

The toy soldiers were sold for £550, and Tommy's shoulders slumped as the glass case was carried away.

Mr Scarrot wished there was something else in the sale that might bring the smile back to Tommy's face but there was nothing suitable for a five year old boy. For the first time he left a sale empty handed.

As they walked back to Mr Scarrot's old white van the door of a large gleaming black car opened and a small plump elderly gentleman stepped out. His pink cheeks were closely shaven and a fringe of silvery white hair was neatly combed above a spotless white shirt and a dark striped suit.

'Young man,' he called to Tommy, and beckoned with a well manicured finger.

Hesitantly Tommy walked towards him and the family saw the old gentleman bend to speak into his upturned face. A short time later he clapped Tommy on the shoulder, climbed into his car and drove away. For a moment Tommy stared after him before he turned and rushed back to Mr Scarrot.

'Look! Look what I've got!' He opened his hand and showed his father a scarlet coated soldier mounted on a white horse. 'He said it was to start my own collection. I gave him a sixpence for it!' With reverence he touched the perfectly formed little soldier with the tip of a finger.

Mr Scarrot calculated. The soldier must be worth a pound or more. He wished he had been able to thank the stranger for his generosity. It was wonderful to see the smile back on Tommy's face.

He looked a bit like Father Christmas, didn't he?' said Tommy as they drove back to Kenmere. 'But I don't suppose he was really. Just looked like him.' He gave the soldier's tiny helmet a final polish and placed him with great care in the pocket of his shirt.

4

Tommy Goes To School

It was Tommy's first day at school. He stood just inside the gates, his back to the playground, and stared hard at a spot where the black paint had peeled away. The metal beneath was bright orange with rust. He examined it for a long time, reluctant to turn around and face the others.

He wished he had asked his Dad to stay with him. Or Jenny. They had both offered but Tommy had told them that he wasn't a baby, thank you very much, and now Dad had gone off to deliver his vegetables and Jenny had rushed away to join her friends in the far corner of the playground.

He was on his own. He stared at the orange patch a moment longer, took a deep breath, squared his shoulders and turned.

There must be a thousand of them! Five thousand! All leaping and skipping, throwing satchels, wrestling and shoving. He waited for them to notice him but no one spared Tommy a glance.

In another few minutes the bell would ring and they would all leave him, alone in the playground. Panic stirred him to action. He gazed about him, selected at random a group of four boys and two girls and marched into their midst.

'I'm Tommy Scarrot,' he announced loudly.

'I live on an island,' he shouted when the group made no reply.

They were not impressed. Islands were two a penny in the Lake District.

'It's called Pineapple Island.'

One of the girls, the red haired one, began to plait the front of her hair into a row of tiny corkscrews. The other turned green eyes, like bright glass beads, upon him and spoke.

'Has it got pineapples on it?'

'Don't be daft,' said a tall tow-haired boy with big hands and scabby knees. He released his headlock on one of the smaller boys and gazed at the girl with scorn. 'Pineapples don't grow in the Lake District. If he says that he's telling fibs.'

'I am not! We have got pineapples.' And so they had, Tommy thought defiantly. There were two tins on the shelf in Mam's kitchen.

'Liar!'

'I'm not!'

'Fibber!'

'I'm not!'

'It's a daft name anyway. Whoever heard of an island called Pinapple Island?'

'Who cares?'

The big boy selected another smaller victim and bent him backwards over one broad knee. The others watched with nervous admiration. Tommy searched his mind for something to draw their attention back to himself. At any moment the bell would ring. What could he talk about? And then he remembered.

'Last Wednesday,' he said slowly. 'Last Wednesday ... I ate a ladybird!'

The big boy let go of his victim so abruptly that the smaller boy fell in a heap at his feet. A hush fell over the group.

'That's cruel!' said the red haired girl.

'Only by accident,' Tommy said hastily.

'What did it taste like?' she asked.

'Bitter. Like iron railings.'

There was another silence while they all thought about iron railings and those who had never tasted one took a lick of the school gates.

'I ate half a caterpillar once,' contributed a small boy with round wire spectacles. 'It was sweet. Like sugar. One of those long thin green ones, it was.'

'My Mam nearly ate a beetle in a loaf once ... '

'I wonder what moths taste like?'

'Like brown paper, I expect.'

Tommy heaved a sigh of relief. It was all right.

The bell rang and the girl with red hair linked her arm in his.

'My name's Deborah Flack,' she told him. 'You can be my friend if you like.'

Tommy didn't like. After all, she was a girl and he had quite enough of girls at home, but it was a start.

The big boy began to force a passage through the crowd and the others followed in his wake. Tommy allowed Deborah to drag him up the steps, along a corridor lined with tall teachers, and into the biggest room he had ever seen. Rows and rows of children sat cross-legged before a platform lined with more teachers. Deborah forced him down beside her on to the splintery wooden floor and told him in a loud whisper that this was Assembly.

Up on the platform one of the teachers began to bang out a hymn on the piano. Deborah dragged him to his feet again.

He sang.

All things bright and beautiful,
All creatures great and small ...

Deborah was singing different words.

Custard thick and fruity full
That makes you strong and tall -

Tommy stared at her in horror. She winked.

Cream cakes, buns and tri-i-fle,
Our grocer has them all ...

Seven hours later Tommy sat in the stern of Mr Scarrot's rowing boat, wedged between Jack and a box of unsold carrots. It had been an interesting day on the whole, he decided. School dinner had been disappointing - tinned meat, mash and string beans - and he had felt a bit of a sissy pretending to be a tree in Music and Movement, but he had enjoyed the finger painting and that game with the pictures and words on cards.

'Well, son,' said Mr Scarrot. 'How did your first day go? Want to go back tomorrow?'

'D'you mean he's got a choice?' asked Poppy from the front of the boat. She had taken to sighing heavily at the prospect of her end of year exams.

'I don't know why you're always complaining,' said Jenny primly. 'I think school's lovely.'

'Wait till you're older,' said Jack in a voice of gloom. 'The only good thing about school is football.'

Tommy trailed his fingers in the water and squinted across Lake Kenmere towards the island. He fancied he could see his mother at the kitchen window. Or was it a pot of flowers?

'Dad. Why is our island called Pineapple Island?'

'I don't know, son. Ask your mother.'

Tommy, who thought his Dad knew everything, was disappointed. But he forgot all about pineapples when he saw the big steak and kidney pie and the fruit cake, heavy with cherries and raisins, that Mrs Scarrot had made for their evening meal.

It was only after he'd blotted up the last sticky crumbs from his plate with the tip of his finger that he remembered.

'Mam, why is our island called Pineapple Island? Dad said to ask you.'

'Ah! Your Dad's good at growing vegetables but he never was one for telling a story. Not that I'm a patch on your Aunt Mabel, mind, but good enough. Well now ... ' She leaned back and picked up her knitting, a pale blue tiny jacket - just about the right size for

Philomena Haggerty, thought Jenny with sudden interest. Mrs Scarrot peered at the tiny garment, re-knitted a couple of dropped stitches and laid it aside. She settled herself in her chair.

'Once upon a time, a hundred years ago, there lived a gentleman by the name of Sir Martin Fitzbudgett - '

'Not *our* Fitzbudgett? The Colonel?' interrupted Tommy.

'Don't be stupid,' said Jenny. 'Ours isn't old enough.'

'He is too. He's *very* old. He's as old as - as old as Moses.'

Mrs Scarrot frowned. She disliked having her stories interrupted.

'The Colonel is Sir Martin's great grandson and nothing to do with it. Now Sir Martin was very wealthy. He owned all the land hereabouts and all the hills and one or two of the lakes, including our lake. In fact, it was on this very island that he kept his aged mother after he married Lady Emmeline, because the two women didn't get on, not one bit.

'One day Sir Martin decided to climb Skirn Pike, that's the big hill that overlooks the lake from the North. He liked climbing, because although he had a very big nose the rest of him was very small, and when he stood on top of a high hill he felt big all over.'

Tommy could understand that. He felt exactly the same when he stood on top of the log pile beside the shed. With sudden anxiety he felt his nose. No, it was all right.

'So Lady Emmeline broke off from her embroidery to make up some sandwiches for him. Camembert and onion, he had - '

'Last time you said it was tuna fish and caviar,' corrected Jenny, who had heard the story before.

Mrs Scarrot ignored the interruption. 'And Sir Martin set off up Skirn Pike with his walking stick and his pith helmet that he had saved from when he was in the Indian Army. When he reached the top he was very glad to sit down and rest while he ate his sandwiches, and while he rested he looked down at all the land that he owned - the green fields and the hills all mauve and blue, and the water that shone like blue gems in the sunshine. And in the middle of one of those blue gems was this island.

'It was then for the first time that Sir Martin noticed its peculiar shape. At that time it was just called Kenmere Island, but the more he looked at it the more its shape reminded him of something. Something that he liked, something that his butler had orders to purchase for him whenever a ship came up the coast from the Tropics. And that something was ... '

'A pineapple!' finished Jenny triumphantly.

'And so, even though Lady Emmeline argued that it was far too exotic a name for the Lake District and even his aged mother thought it was a bit silly and she would have to have all her notepaper reprinted, that's what Sir Martin called it. And Pineapple Island it's been ever since.'

With a smile of satisfaction Mrs Scarrot went back to her knitting, Jenny went off to measure Philomena's chest size, and the two older children disappeared to their bedrooms to do homework.

Well! That wasn't much of a story, thought Tommy as he wandered down to the little wooden jetty at the water's edge and sat down, his legs dangling above the water. Not enough to impress anyone at school. It would be much better if... if...

At the end of half an hour he had concocted a much more exciting explanation. Of galleons and tropic seas and a mutiny. And pirates, and a desperate flight to a little island in the Lake District with a precious cargo of pineapples. And how they barricaded themselves against the British Navy behind boxes and boxes of pineapples and how they lived off pineapples and water until all but one had died and that one's name was Scarrot. Yes, that was much better.

But how did they get the galleon across from the sea to the lake? Oh dear ... He would have to start all over.

5

New Arrivals

One morning a few weeks later, Charlie arrived. He came in that noisy hour just before dawn when all the birds are waking up and clearing their throats to sing.

No one was expecting him, least of all Mrs Scarrot. Mr Scarrot was snatched from a dream of being pummelled by a boxing kangaroo to find that he was being pummelled by Mrs Scarrot.

'Fred!' she hissed. 'I think it's Charlie!'

Mr Scarrot sighed and rubbed his eyes. 'I'll get the boat,' he mumbled and sank back into sleep.

'I don't think there's time!'

Mr Scarrot leapt out of bed and backed towards the door.

'Well, er ... What shall I do?' He turned around in a helpless circle. 'Er - oh, hot water, that's it! I'll get you some hot water.'

'I'd rather have a cup of tea.'

At this point you might ask why Mrs Scarrot was so sure that it would be Charlie and not, say, Susan or Jessica or Caroline. Well, there is no answer to that. Mrs Scarrot just knew. And she was right, for when the children crept into their parents' bedroom just before breakfast, there was Charlie.

He should have waited another two weeks until Mrs Scarrot was installed in hospital with two nurses beside her, her best pink and white bed jacket around her shoulders and a basket of fruit on the bedside cabinet, but then that was Charlie. Always in the wrong place at the wrong time, always turning the best laid plans topsy turvy and leaving chaos behind him. The children thought he was wonderful.

'When can we hold him?' Jenny laid a finger against his cheek. Charlie screwed up his tiny face in a ferocious gesture and she jumped back.

'Soon,' said Mrs Scarrot. 'When he's not quite so fragile.'

Each day the children asked, until at last she decided that perhaps Charlie was old enough and strong enough to withstand their enthusiasm. With some misgivings and many warnings, she let them hold him.

She need not have worried. It was the children who suffered, not Charlie, for as they hugged and kissed him, passing him from one to another, Charlie left behind a trail of damp laps, broken necklaces, pulled out hair, bent spectacles and torn off buttons.

Charlie, it was clear, was destined to make his mark on the world.

What on earth would they do, Mrs Scarrot wondered, when he could get about by himself? Already his small bright eyes were everywhere, planning mischief.

'You're going to be a terror!' she told him, half scolding. Charlie gave her his toothless happy smile and she nuzzled his neck, pushing the future away.

But Charlie soon learned to crawl and quickly fulfilled the worst of Mrs Scarrot's forebodings. So that when the letter arrived from Grandma and Grampa saying they had at last sold their grocery shop in Slough and were coming to the island, her first thought (although she was ashamed to admit it) was: Thank goodness, two more pairs of hands to look after Charlie! For six people were just not enough. Charlie could quite easily be in seven or even eight places at once. Sometimes it seemed that Charlie was everywhere.

The next two weeks were busy ones, with Mr Scarrot building another extension and Mrs Scarrot sewing curtains and bedcovers in readiness for the grandparents' arrival. The curtains were green, patterned with large pink peonies. She hoped Grandma would like them. Personally, she was sick of peonies. Mr Scarrot had bought a 100 yard bale of the material at a sale and it was all she could do to use it up. Everything, even Charlie's play overalls, was covered in peonies.

It was raining when Mr Scarrot set off to fetch Grandma and Grampa from the station. Mrs Scarrot and the children waited at home on the island. Every five minutes one of them peered across the lake, until at five o'clock Jack gave a great shout as he made out through the grey curtain of rain the outline of the raft approaching the island.

They all rushed outside and watched Mr Scarrot punt the raft towards the jetty. His feet were surrounded by boxes and crates, and in the centre of the raft two small erect figures shared a large black umbrella.

Grandma and Grampa had arrived.

As soon as she set foot on the island Grandma began to talk, a rush of breathless conversation that poured over the Scarrots in an unstoppable torrent. How big the children had grown, she said, why Jenny and Tommy were only babies when - and Charlie, oh, what a little lamb, and what a bright house - how unusual, all those different colours - how long had Jenny been wearing glasses? - and, my goodness, how pretty Poppy was, just like Fred's Auntie Grace, the one who went off with you-know-who. She hugged and kissed everyone within range, spectacles askew on her nose, black straw hat aslant over one eye, and as Mr Scarrot and Jack unloaded boxes off the raft, went round them all again, finishing with Charlie, who stared at her entranced from the circle of her arms, making no attempt to compete with such a delightfully noisy lady.

Grampa was used to Grandma's talking. He waited, thumbs stuck in the pockets of his bulging waistcoat.

Tommy stole glances at him. It was three years since they had visited Slough and the only memories that remained were of

Grampa's pipe, which had smelled like the time his Dad had burned a rubber tyre on the bonfire, and Grandma's hat, a bright green feathered thing which had remained jammed on her head throughout the very large tea they had eaten in the little sitting room behind the shop.

He thought Grampa looked interesting. He looked like a nice apple, small and round and rosy, and his hair was white and wispy. The top of his head shone through, like pink china. His eyebrows were very thick and bushy and when he saw Tommy watching him, he wriggled them like caterpillars. For a moment he looked quite fierce, but then he held out his arms and smiled. It was Charlie's smile, wide and toothless. With an answering grin, Tommy ran to him.

Mr Scarrot and Jack were still carrying boxes into the house.

'The people who bought the shop didn't want the stock,' Grandma explained. 'They're turning it into a coffee bar, so we brought everything with us.'

'You should have seen the train!' said Mr Scarrot, pausing to wipe his brow with a large red handkerchief. 'I've never seen anything like it. We filled half a goods van!'

'But ... ' Mrs Scarrot stared around her kitchen, that was beginning to look like a warehouse. 'Where am I going to put it all?'

'I can always build another extension,' said Mr Scarrot hopefully.

That night when the Scarrot family sat down to supper the table groaned with food. There were pork pies, veal pies, ham and egg pies; jellies and fruit tarts, chocolate biscuits and five kinds of cake; there was Gentleman's Relish which the children liked and Pate de Fois Gras which they didn't; there were thick pink slices of ham and thin brown slices of beef; there were three different cheeses and four kinds of pickle. And finally, in the centre of the table, was the special cake that Mrs Scarrot had baked in celebration. A large square fruit cake covered with pink icing edged with red sugar roses, and the words *Welcome to Grampa and Grandma* in bright green across the centre.

They ate and ate and ate. Cheeks bulged, eyes glazed and stomachs tightened like drums, but at last they all had to admit that they could eat not one more mouthful, not one single crumb, not even a taste of that mouthwatering strawberry shortcake or the tiniest smidgeon of bakewell tart.

'Where's Charlie' asked Mrs Scarrot as she unzipped her skirt so that she could breathe again. 'It's time he went to bed.'

Charlie's high chair was empty, except for two half-eaten chocolate biscuits and a spat-out lump of pork pie.

'Oh dear,' sighed Mrs Scarrot. 'He's gone again.'

'It's all right, Alice,' said Grandma. 'He's under the table, by my feet.'

And there was Charlie, curled up on the floor between Grandma's shiny black lace-ups, one sticky hand clasping her bunion. The other clutched a crumbling slice of cake, and a wide jammy smile was smeared across his face. He was fast asleep.

6

Where's Grandma?

There was no doubt about it. Grandma was a talker. It was only in the early morning that you could hold a reasonable conversation with her. After that she would wind herself up like an old-fashioned gramophone until by teatime it was difficult to squeeze in half a sentence between her breathless monologues.

The reason for all this non-stop chatter was Grandma's deafness. Although she wore a hearing aid and could hear quite well when it was correctly adjusted, she couldn't resist playing with the volume knob. In the middle of a perfectly good conversation she would twiddle until the words rose to the wailing shriek of a fire engine speeding to a fire, or faded away like the low gurgling murmur of water down a plug hole. Once that happened, Grandma could never get it quite right again, and in the end she would give up altogether, turn the darn thing off and just talk.

Anyway, she would say, what was there to listen to any more? In seventy years she reckoned she had heard it all at least ten times over!

Sometimes Poppy, who had the bedroom next to Jack's, wished that she, like Grandma, could have silence just by the click of a switch. Because Jack had given up football completely and was now concentrating on becoming a rock star.

She could never quite decide which was worse: Jack practising on his guitar or Jack stamping the floor, slapping his sides and howling into his microphone (which was not a real microphone, just a floor mop borrowed from Mrs Scarrot). Both were hard to bear in a wooden house where even the smallest noise at one end could be heard at the other.

The more Jack practised, the more bloodcurdling became the howls and shrieks that filtered through his bedroom walls, until at last, after Tommy had pleaded for Mr Scarrot to please please find the poor sick animal and help it, Mr Scarrot decided to build a special extension just for Jack. A soundproof music room.

He took a day off from his vegetables to think about it. If he built double walls fifteen inches apart and packed the space between with straw, that would do the job. And if he insulated the roof as well, it would be even better. Once inside, Jack could make as much noise as he liked and no one need suffer.

At the news that he was to have his very own music room Jack swelled with pride. (No one had told him the real reason: in spite of everything, they were all quite fond of him). Jack decided that the least he could do was to put aside his guitar for a week and help his father.

Mr Scarrot had almost finished the fourth wall when he realised to his dismay that the plank of wood he had just picked up was the last. No matter how carefully he and Jack scoured the island they could find no more. He would have to go and buy some from the nearest timber yard. It was then two o'clock in the afternoon. It would take at least two hours there and back.

'If you're going to town I'll come with you, Dad,' said Poppy. 'I'd like to change my library books.'

'And I need some more sugar for jam making,' said Mrs Scarrot.

For once, Grandma's hearing aid was switched on and adjusted.

'Why don't you both go?' she urged. 'You too, Grampa. You can go to the library with Poppy. You can get me that book that I was reading before we moved. You know, the one where she meets a duke who's pretending to be a jockey and he meets this princess, only she's not really a princess but the poor daughter of a diamond merchant who's lost all his money to a vicar who isn't really a vicar, and he can't decide between the first one, who's sworn she'll never marry but really she's head over heels ... '

'I don't think Jenny and Tommy will want to come,' said Mrs Scarrot. 'They've got something planned for this afternoon.'

'Leave them here, then,' said Grandma. 'I'll look after them. And Charlie too. You go out and enjoy yourself for a change.'

Mrs Scarrot was pleased to accept her offer, and ten minutes later the raft set off with Mr and Mrs Scarrot, Grampa, Jack and Poppy aboard.

'Me and Jenny are going to build a dam across the stream,' announced Tommy when they had gone.

'Well, I suppose that's all right. As long as you don't fall in,' said Grandma.

Tommy gave her his patient look. As if they would. Only little children fell into streams.

'It's not very deep,' said Jenny. 'And I'll look after Tommy,' she added, ignoring his indignant snort.

Grandma took a folding chair out to the front porch, choosing a spot where her head was shaded but a warm shaft of sunlight fell across her legs and feet, which always seemed to feel the cold nowadays. She was knitting a jumper for Jenny, in a nice shade called Honey Gold to go with her hair. Now and then she glanced across at Charlie, who was exercising on the grass in front of her. It was amazing how quickly he could crawl. Round and round the circular lawn, elbows and knees working with the speed of piston rods in an engine. She smiled fondly as he paused to inspect a snail at ground level, his small button nose almost touching the round brown shell.

It was a lovely day, she decided dreamily, with everything as it should be. Jenny and Tommy by the stream, Charlie on the lawn, God in his Heaven and all right with the world. A lovely day ...

She was sure she had only closed her eyes for a second, but when she awoke Charlie had disappeared. In the distance she could hear the voices of Jenny and Tommy as they played by the stream.

'Oh dear!' She hoped Charlie had not crawled towards the water. As quickly as she could, she hobbled to the bottom of the garden.

'Have you seen Charlie?'

Jenny and Tommy shook their heads.

'Try the kitchen,' Jenny suggested. 'He often crawls in there now. He climbs in the bread bin after the bread.'

Grandma looked in the kitchen and in all the other rooms. No Charlie. Worried now, she hurried outside again.

'Charlie?' She circled the house. 'Charlie?' she called, and heard an answering chortle.

'Charlie, where are you, you naughty boy?'

He chortled again and then she saw that he had crawled between the unfinished sections of the music room wall and was sitting at the far end, gnawing on a large hunk of bread.

'Charlie! Come out of there at once!'

But Charlie ignored her and continued to gnash on his crust.

Grandma glared at him. 'Charlie!'

Charlie sucked noisily.

Grandma's heart sank. She would have to go in and fetch him. There was no choice. Taking a deep breath and making herself as thin as she could, she squeezed into the gap between the walls.

Down by the stream Jenny sat back on her heels and listened.

'Grandma's not calling any more.'

'I expect she's found him.' Tommy was more concerned with the trickle of water that was still getting through the dam. 'Should we put another row of stones here, d'you think?'

Jenny contemplated the oozing barrier. 'Dad's got some cement in his workshop.'

It was a lovely idea but Tommy shook his head. 'He'd be awfully mad if we touched that.'

Five miles away in Windermere Mr Scarrot had bought his timber.

He and Jack had lashed it to the roof rack on top of the van and were now leaning against the van eating ice cream cornets as they waited for the others.

'Here they come', said Jack.

'Ooh, ice cream. Where's ours?' asked Poppy.

'Never mind ice cream,' said Grampa. 'Let's all go and have a cream tea. My treat.'

Mrs Scarrot had not even peeled the potatoes for their evening meal before they left the island. She looked at her watch, but the thought of scones and cream and home made strawberry jam at the little Tea Shoppe by the lake was just too tempting.

'Well, thank you, Grampa. That'd be lovely, really lovely.'

Back on the island Grandma was stuck. While Charlie chortled and gurgled, she heaved and pushed but it was useless. She had been within a hand's grab of the child when Mr Scarrot's walls, crooked as always, narrowed and Grandma could go no further. Worse, she found that she could not retreat either. She called to Tommy and Jenny but they were too far away.

Well, she decided at last, after she had bruised both elbows, laddered her stockings and lost three buttons from her cardigan, all she could do was wait until help came. At least she knew where Charlie was. With one last effort she managed to squirm into a sitting position, then absently she twiddled with her hearing aid and as the blessed silence surrounded her, her eyelids drooped, her chin sank to her chest and she slept.

Later, having finished his bread and sucked the last soggy crumbs from his fingers Charlie poked Grandma's nose. She gave forth a gentle snore. Chuckling, he poked it again but this time there was no response. After a few moments, accepting that Grandma was not going to play with him, he scrambled over her sleeping body, crawled along the gap and was away.

It was nearly six o'clock when the others returned to the island. Mrs Scarrot hurried straight to the kitchen. She had planned a nice stew with dumplings but it was too late for that now. It would have to be bacon and egg pie with fried potatoes, cabbage and green beans. She set Poppy and Jack to work peeling potatoes while she washed the vegetables, chopped bacon and weighed flour.

There was no time to worry about the younger ones. Grandma wouldn't mind looking after them for a little longer. When Charlie crawled into the kitchen and peered up at her with a soil-smeared face she continued to rub fat into flour as she talked to him with the half-loving, half-scolding note in her voice that Charlie so often brought out.

'Eh, just look at you. You've been at your Dad's seed bed again, haven't you, little rapscallion! Gave Grandma the slip, I suppose.' She pushed her sleeves a little higher and began to roll out the pastry with a large blue and white china rolling pin. 'Poppy, love, wash his hands and face, will you. Oh, just look at your knees, you naughty boy, another pair of overalls ruined. Thank goodness for the material your Dad bought, even if I am sick of it!'

'Hello, Mam.' It was Jenny and Tommy, looking tired but triumphant. 'We've built a lovely dam.'

'That's nice, dears. I'll have a look after dinner. Now leave that alone,' she said as Tommy filched a lump of pastry. 'How you can eat it uncooked I don't know. It would lie like lead on my stomach.' She took the dish away from him and bustled over to the oven. 'There, another half hour and dinner will be ready.'

Mr Scarrot poked his head around the door. 'If there's half an hour to spare I think I'll just finish that wall. Shouldn't take long, just needs half a dozen planks.'

Grampa wandered in and out of the kitchen, wondering where Grandma could have got to. He had looked in their bedroom and he had called her once or twice in the garden but he guessed she had switched off her hearing aid. Never mind, he thought, picking up his new library book and sinking into a chair in the sitting room, she would come back for dinner, she always did. Grandma's hearing might be a bit the worse for wear but there was nothing wrong with her appetite.

In half an hour Mrs Scarrot took the pie out of the oven and carried it, steaming and golden, into the dining room. Poppy followed with the dish of fried potatoes, Jenny carried the beans and Tommy the bowl of pale green cabbage. He wrinkled his nose and averted his eyes. If there was one thing he hated it was cabbage. If someone offered him a thousand pounds - or better still, a bicycle - he would still hate it.

'Dinner's ready, everyone.' Mrs Scarrot dealt out plates on the table with one hand and heaved Charlie into his high chair with the other.

'Where's Grandma?' she asked, when everyone was seated.

Mr Scarrot looked at Grampa, Poppy looked at Jack, Jenny looked at Tommy, and Charlie seized the opportunity to lean over the side of his chair and stab a finger into the bacon and egg pie.

'She was looking for Charlie last time we saw her,' said Jenny.

'But Charlie's here.'

Mr Scarrot sighed. 'Put my plate back in the oven, Alice, and I'll go and fetch her. She's most likely switched off her hearing aid and forgotten the time.'

In ten minutes he was back. 'I've been all over the island, but I can't see her anywhere.'

Mrs Scarrot stared at him. 'But she must be somewhere. Look, you stay here with Grampa and eat your dinner. The children and I will look again.'

By the time Mr Scarrot had finished his meal the sun was setting and Grandma had still not been found.

'Perhaps she's drowned,' Tommy said, his lower lip trembling. 'Perhaps she's drowned in the stream after we dammed it!'

'Don't be silly,' Poppy said. 'Grandma's got too much sense to drown.'

'Then where is she?' asked Jack.

They were grouped outside the house, and as if in answer to his question there came a strange snorting noise from close at hand. It was followed by a squeak and a snuffle and a dull thump. Jenny moved closer to Mr Scarrot, thinking it sounded rather like a bear awakening from its winter hibernation.

'What was that?' asked Mrs Scarrot.

'Fred? Grampa? Get me out!' The voice was faint and muffled.

It was Grandma's voice, but where was she?

The thumps came again, louder, and Mr Scarrot's jaw dropped. 'She's in the wall! She's inside my wall!'

'Oh, Fred,' Mrs Scarrot reproached him. She shook her head. 'Oh, Fred!'

Mr Scarrot took a step backwards. He looked round at the others, who were all shaking their heads now. 'Well, how was I to know?'

It was a cross and ruffled Grandma who staggered out into the garden after Mr Scarrot had dismantled half the wall. She stared around her and her nose twitched as the family fussed over her, dusting her down and straightening her clothes.

'I can smell bacon and egg pie,' she accused. 'And fried potatoes. You've all eaten without me!'

She rounded on Mr Scarrot, who was plucking wood shavings from her hair, and slapped his hand away.

'Darn you, Fred,' she snapped. 'You've made me miss my dinner!'

7

The Teller of Tales

The long golden drought that had lasted all through July broke at last and the skies were full of purple clouds when Aunt Mabel's varicose veins brought her and Uncle Arthur to Pineapple Island.

'My legs just wouldn't stand it no more,' she told Mrs Scarrot cheerfully. 'My doctor said if I didn't give up the pub he'd wash his hands off them!'

Tommy and Jenny stole a glance at Aunt Mabel's legs in their thick elastic stockings. They couldn't see anything wrong with them, not from the outside anyway. They couldn't see anything wrong with Aunt Mabel at all. She was, in fact, the most glamorous creature they had ever seen.

With dazzled eyes they gazed at her shining golden yellow hair, a magnificent towering structure a full twelve inches high that swayed from side to side as she moved. They stared at her glossy scarlet lips and the incredible inch-long eyelashes that framed her china blue eyes like thick black fluttering fringes ('They come off,' Jenny whispered to Tommy a week later in their secret place behind Mr Scarrot's workshop. 'I saw them lying on her dressing table!') and they stared at the two huge golden hearts that hung jingle-jangling from her ear lobes, and the plump white hands with long crimson fingernails and nine rings, and the shiny white mackintosh printed with yellow daisies that matched the bright yellow of her umbrella.

She was as beautiful as a princess, thought Jenny. Tommy decided it was lucky Aunt Mabel had very coarse veins and had to give up the pub. If her veins had not been so coarse she might never have come to live with them on the island!

Overwhelmed by Aunt Mabel's presence they hardly noticed Uncle Arthur. But then, Uncle Arthur was such a quiet person. Quiet and thin. Thin face, a thin tattered moustache that covered his mouth, thin hair that did a less successful job on his head, a thin body in a quiet grey suit. He smiled at the children but didn't speak.

In the weeks and months that followed they never did hear him speak. Once Poppy was heard to remark that she didn't believe he *could* speak. This made Aunt Mabel quite cross. He spoke to *her*, she said, and after that she made a point of repeating snippets of his conversation which were truly brilliant (Uncle Arthur was obviously a very clever man) but still no one else heard him utter a word. He just smiled.

It was hard to believe that such a silent man had once swept Aunt Mabel off her feet and whisked her away from a dazzling career on the stage, but perhaps if he had not, perhaps if Aunt Mabel had gone on to become a famous dancer instead of a pub landlady, she would now be somewhere else - in Paris or New York or Las Vegas - instead of Pineapple Island. So perhaps Jenny and Tommy had reason to be grateful to him.

In the bedroom that Uncle Arthur and Aunt Mabel occupied there was a large chest. Old and battered, covered in faded labels addressed to long forgotten theatres, it was the sort of chest you would still find in many a shabby backstage dressing room. Inside the chest were Aunt Mabel's souvenirs, and at the drop of a hat Aunt Mabel would choose one and weave a story around it, transporting the children from Pineapple Island to a different world and a different time, ten, twenty or thirty years ago. For Aunt Mabel was that rare being, a teller of tales.

One day she told Poppy, Jack, Jenny and Tommy the tale of how Uncle Arthur had whisked her away from the stage.

It was four o'clock on a Friday afternoon. It had rained without ceasing for a week, lashing against the windows and drumming on the roof of the wooden house. The wind was from the east and Mr Scarrot had placed a bucket beneath the leak in the hall ceiling, but inside Aunt Mabel's and Uncle Arthur's bedroom the lamps were lit against the early gloom.

'What's this, Aunt Mabel?' Poppy, kneeling beside the open chest, had lifted out a small silver photograph frame. Inside the frame, where there would have been a picture, was a single pressed flower. It was the palest pink, its colour faded almost to transparency, and the edges of the petals were brown and jagged.

'Ah yes.' Aunt Mabel took the frame and her face softened. 'This may look to you just an ordinary flower, but it's got a very special history.' She stared at it for a long time. 'Nearly thirty years ago, it was. Your Uncle Arthur was very handsome then.'

The children stared at Uncle Arthur, who was asleep in the corner armchair. He slept, as he did everything else, without a sound, but his breath fluttered the ragged edges of his moustache.

'I told you about being an orphan, didn't I?'

The children nodded.

'My father's older sister, Aunt Joanna, was my guardian. She didn't like me dancing on the stage but she liked your Uncle Arthur even less and I was only nineteen then, too young at that time to be married without her permission.'

The children listened as she described the bitter arguments, the tears and pleas as the young couple tried to win Aunt Joanna's approval of the marriage. In the end, Aunt Mabel said, they decided to elope to Gretna Green, which was a famous village in Scotland where young people who were still under age could marry.

'We saved and saved,' she said. 'Every penny, because we would have to live there for three weeks before the wedding. We were full of plans and so happy but ... There was one thing that upset me, one problem that I wished I could solve. I was dancing in the chorus line of a new musical, 'Paris Holiday' it was called, and I even had my own little solo, just a few steps and a pirouette, but all on my own. I knew that if I left the show before the end of the run without a very good reason then I would never get another job in the theatre.'

Jenny gripped Poppy's hand. Oh, poor Aunt Mabel!

'But what could I do? I couldn't tell anyone or it might get back to Aunt Joanna. Well, I loved your Uncle Arthur and that was more important than anything, so I tried to put out of my head all thoughts of never dancing again.

'And then - then I heard that on the very night Uncle Arthur and I were planning to run away, the Queen was coming to see the show and afterwards we were all to be presented to her. Oh children, you can't imagine how I felt! It was something we'd all dreamed about, and I would be dancing my first solo! But afterwards ... ' Aunt Mabel stroked the glass over the faded flower. 'Afterwards Arthur and I were catching the midnight train to Scotland. If I stayed to be presented to Her Majesty, then we would miss the train and all our plans would fall apart.'

'Oh, Aunt Mabel.' Jenny moaned in sympathy.

'Well, we went ahead with our preparations, and on the night itself - You should have seen the theatre, Poppy. Everything shined and polished, the foyer full of flowers, new carpet ... And the Royal Box, glittering blue and gold and white. Backstage we were all so excited, and Anna Fairfax, the star of the show, was having hysterics ... '

'Go on, Aunt Mabel,' Tommy urged. 'What happened?'

Aunt Mabel smiled,. 'Well, I saw the Queen. We all peeped through the curtain before the show started and I saw her in the Royal Box. She looked so beautiful. She wore a long pale blue lace dress, and the diamonds in her tiara shone like all the stars in the sky. She looked down and smiled that lovely smile of hers, and there was a great sigh from the audience. They all loved her.

'And then the orchestra broke into the overture and the show was on. It was wonderful. The whole cast performed as they'd never performed before and I - I danced for the Queen! I'll never forget it.'

Aunt Mabel closed her eyes, remembering. She remembered for

so long that Tommy thought she might have gone to sleep. He gave her a gentle nudge and her eyes opened.

'When it was all over and everyone was getting ready for the Royal presentation I changed into my travelling clothes and got my case from the cupboard where I'd hidden it. And then - there was hardly time but I couldn't resist it - I sneaked up to the Royal box. Oh, she'd gone, of course, but I just wanted to see it, to imagine ... It was empty as I expected, but as I was turning to leave I saw, there on the blue carpet, a single flower. *This* flower,' said Aunt Mabel, pointing to the picture frame. 'It had fallen from the Queen's bouquet. It was bright pink then, fresh and fragrant. I picked it up and I pinned it to my jacket.'

She stared at the faded flower in its frame and then, gently, she put it back in the chest.

She smiled at the children. 'You'll probably think it silly,' she said, 'but all the way to Scotland, on that long dark journey through the night, I touched and smelled that flower and I pretended that the Queen had presented it to me herself. And do you know?' She gave her lovely fat chuckle and ruffled Tommy's hair. 'By the time we got to Scotland I almost believed it!'

8

Jack's First Concert

Jack had a new suit. Mrs Scarrot had made it for him on her old treadle sewing machine. It was no ordinary suit. Made of dark blue satin with silver braid swirling around the collar and cuffs, it was a suit for a rock star and Jack struck a proud pose before the long mirror that Mr Scarrot had bought at a sale and put up, after much pleading from Jack, in the Music Room.

The suit was copied from one that his idol, Elvis Presley, had worn. Jack gazed at himself with admiration.

Today was a very special day, a red letter day, the start of his career. After dinner that evening Jack was giving his first public performance. He had invited the Colonel, Mr and Mrs Firbank and the Peabodys to come and listen. It was a shame that all of them had other commitments and wouldn't be able to attend, but it was still going to be a proper concert, with the family all sitting in rows and a little platform for himself in front of the sitting room window. It would have been nice to have a real microphone, though. Two weeks ago he had asked Mr Scarrot to look out for one at the auctions, but his Dad had told him that he'd never seen such things sold secondhand.

Jack had been practising all day for the concert, refusing to come out of the Music Room even for lunch.

'Are you all right?' Poppy asked when she went back to the Music Room and saw he had eaten only one of the sandwiches she had left for him earlier.

'I'm fine,' said Jack. 'Poppy, listen to this.'

He struck a chord on his guitar and let out a high-pitched howl. Poppy edged towards the door. He struck a second chord and gave another bloodcurdling howl. 'Which sounds better?'

Poppy thought they both sounded dreadful. 'The second,' she said.

Jack smiled smugly. 'I thought so too.'

Poppy took a bite out of one of the sandwiches as she carried the plate back to the kitchen. It was good. Beef and horseradish, her favourite. She finished the sandwich and took another. After all, lunch was nearly an hour ago.

'Mam, do I really have to be there tonight? I'd much rather have a bath and wash my hair.'

'So would we all, Poppy, but it would hardly be fair, would it? We have to give the poor lad some encouragement - especially as all our neighbours by some strange coincidence have appointments elsewhere!'

Poppy sighed. 'I suppose so, but I don't know what we've done to deserve a budding rock star in the family.'

Mrs Scarrot laughed. 'It will only last an hour or so. Anyway, maybe he'll have improved. He's certainly been practising enough.'

At five o'clock Jenny appeared.

'Mam, I've an awful lot of homework. I really should finish it tonight,' she said.

Mrs Scarrot put down the silver pepper pot she had been polishing. 'Why, Jenny Scarrot, you told me yesterday you'd done every scrap of your homework!'

'I forgot my History. I have to do an essay on Charles the First.'

'Well, Charles the First will have to wait until tomorrow.'

'Tomorrow it's my turn to dig over the chicken run.'

'I'm sure Jack won't mind changing weeks with you.' Mrs Scarrot left no room for argument.

Defeated, Jenny turned away. 'All right, but if I get split eardrums it will be *your* fault.'

Half an hour later it was Tommy. He hovered in the doorway of the dining room as Mrs Scarrot was setting the table. His face was woebegone and his hands clutched his stomach.

'I've got tummy ache.'

It might have worked had not Mrs Scarrot glanced out of the window less than five minutes ago and seen him leaping on and off the woodpile. She straightened the tablecloth and moved the bowl of marigolds across to the sideboard.

'You'd better not have any dinner in that case.' She sighed. 'A pity, it's your favourite tonight. Chicken Maryland with fried bananas and corn fritters.'

There was a long pause.

'I think I might manage just a little. I think my tummy ache might be better by then.'

Mrs Scarrot turned away to hide a smile. 'That's good,' she said. 'It would be a shame to be ill when we're all so looking forward to the concert.'

At six o'clock Jack emerged from the Music Room. His face was haggard.

'Come and have some dinner.' Mrs Scarrot was firm. 'It's Chicken Maryland.'

Jack ate his chicken as if it were sawdust, stopping between bites to hum snatches of music.

Grampa watched him. 'It'll be fine, Jack. Don't be nervous.'

'I'm not nervous.'

'Of course you are,' said Aunt Mabel. 'Professionals are always nervous before a performance.'

Jack smiled but he still picked at his chicken.

After dinner he rushed off to the sitting room to arrange the chairs.

'I can do that,' Mr Scarrot protested.

'No, I'll do it. I want them just right.' Jack heaved at the big sofa, in his haste sweeping a china vase off the side table. Mr Scarrot looked away. Well, it was Jack's night. What if he did break a few ornaments? There were plenty more at the sales.

At seven everything was ready. The big sofa and the armchairs had been pushed back to the walls and in their place were two rows of folding chairs. All the lights were focussed on the little wooden stage that Mr Scarrot had built, and on the curtain behind it Jack had pinned a large hand written poster advertising: 'Jackie Quicksilver - King of Rock!'

As the family filed into their seats Mr Scarrot went along to the Music Room and knocked on the door. 'Ready, Jack?'

Jack picked up his guitar. His hands were damp and his throat was dry but he knew he looked good.

'Ready, Dad,' he said.

'And now,' said Mr Scarrot as he faced the two rows of chairs. 'The man you've been waiting for! Your own, your very own... Jackie Quicksilver!'

The family applauded and Jack strode in, satin suit gleaming in the light of the lamps, guitar slung around his neck on a new scarlet braid strap. He took up his position in front of the microphone (failing a real one, Jack had borrowed one of Tommy's small boxing gloves, bound it to the top of a broomstick and sprayed it silver), waited for the applause to die, flung back his hair, braced his feet apart and raised one hand high in the air, just as he had practised in front of his mirror. Silently he counted three, then brought his hand down in a crashing chord on his guitar.

'Ah hear yuh, baby ... STRUM!

'Ah see yuh, baby ... STRUM, STRUM!

And ah want yuh ...

By mah si-i-ide ... ' STRUM, STRUM, STRUM!

Grandma smiled and nodded her approval, watched with envy by the others, who knew she had switched off her hearing aid. A pained expression came to Grampa's face as Jack let out a wild scream, and Tommy swallowed a hardly sucked humbug with a gulp. Charlie on Mrs Scarrot's knee crowed with delight.

'Ah need yuh -

Cos you're mah - '

Breath held and nerves quivering, the audience waited. The next note was bound to be a high one and their ears flinched in anticipation. But there was silence. They looked at Jack in astonishment. He stared back, equally astonished. He tried again.

'Cos you're mah - '

And then a very strange noise emerged from Jack's open mouth.

'Wo-o-o-!'

Mrs Scarrot bit her lip and stared hard at the top of Charlie's golden head, Aunt Mabel's smile fixed itself even more firmly, and Jack did a quick run of notes on the guitar to cover his confusion.

'Wo-o-o - '

The sound was a deep bray, with an unexpected squeak in the middle. Jack's mouth snapped shut and he stared with helpless embarrassment at his audience. Worst of all was the sight of Mr Scarrot grinning, *grinning*, right in the front row. A miserable sense of betrayal pricked the back of Jack's eyes.

Mr Scarrot jumped up on to the stage. 'It's all right, lad. Nothing to worry about at all. You know what's happened, don't you?'

Jack shook his head.

'Your voice has broken. Give it a rest for a little while and it'll be better than ever.' Mr Scarrot put his arm around Jack's shoulders and gave him a hug. 'Reckon you've got a real good chance of becoming a star now,' he said. 'You'll have a proper man's voice soon, and then - well, the sky's the limit, son!'

Jack gazed into the future. Perhaps his Dad was right. Perhaps soon he would be singing better than ever, and then ... .

His chest swelled and he struck a tremendous chord on his guitar.

Look out, world, here I come!

9

A Sticky Escape

Tommy and Frankie Filkin stopped by the window of the camping shop and pressed envious noses against the glass. They had been first out of school, elbowing and shoving their way through the cloakroom, across the playground and out of the gates, and now they had a full half hour before Tommy had to meet his Dad and the others.

Frankie Filkin lived just five minutes walk from the school but he never went straight home, even though he had his own front door key and the house was empty.

Frankie was rich. His mother owned the Lakeside Gift Shop and gave him a pound a day, besides his dinner money, to spend on anything he liked. He spent a lot of it on best friends. Frankie had more best friends than anyone else in the class. He went through best friends like a rabbit through a row of lettuces. It was not that anyone liked him very much, but they all knew that if you could stick it out for a week, on Friday Frankie would buy you a present.

His best friend this week was Tommy. And today was Friday.

The camping shop window was piled high with an amazing assortment of objects.

'It's not fair,' said Tommy. 'Only visitors go camping. Why can't people who live here camp?' He lifted his shoulders in a sigh. 'It's not fair.'

'What's to stop you going?' asked Frankie.

'Haven't got a tent. My Dad says, what d'you want a tent for when we've got a nice house? He says, better to have a little extension. A '*play room!*' he added.

'I wouldn't mind a play room. You could have a gang in on Saturdays and have a password.'

'It's not the same. You can't take a play room up a mountain or down by a lake and sit round a bonfire with no one to tell you when to go to bed or get up.'

Frankie stared at a small orange tent in the back of the window. Sleeps Two, it said.

'If you promise to stay best friends, I reckon I could get my Mam to buy that tent,' he said. 'And then we could go off at weekends. Wherever you liked.'

'My Dad wouldn't let me anyway. Not without someone older.'

'You could tell him my big brother's going.'

'You haven't got a big brother.'

'Well, your Dad wouldn't know that, would he?'

'My Dad knows everything. Anyway, I bet your Mam wouldn't buy it.'

'She would,' Frankie insisted. 'Mind, you'd have to *promise* to stay best friends, cut your throat and hope to die.'

Tommy's eyes narrowed. 'We'd need a groundsheet. And sleeping bags. And billy cans and matches and tin mugs. We could make dampers in the fire like in that book, you know? You mix flour and water and wrap it round a stick.'

'We could take tins of baked beans and cling peaches and evap,' said Frankie. 'And chocolate - mountaineers always take chocolate - and biscuits and pork pies, and my Mam could make us a fruit cake. And apples and bacon and currant loaf and cheese and ... '

Tommy sighed. That was the trouble with Frankie. He was always talking about food.

'Well, I don't think she'd buy it. It's too dear.'

Frankie grabbed his arm. 'She would, she would. If you promise.'

Tommy said nothing.

'Just for a month,' pleaded Frankie. 'A month would do.'

Tommy stuck his hands in his pockets. 'I'll think about it.'

Frankie sighed with relief. It was enough. 'I'm going to buy your present now.'

Tommy glanced at the camping shop window. He wouldn't mind one of those knife things that opened up and did everything.

'I'm going to buy you a giant cream meringue,' Frankie announced. 'C'mon.'

The meringues were giant, all right. Too big to fit in Tommy's hand.

'My Mam doesn't like me eating sugary things between meals,' he said. 'She says it rots your teeth away to nothing.'

'Go on!' Frankie scoffed, taking such an enormous bite of his meringue that the cream squeezed out either side. 'Nothing wrong with mine, is there?' He flashed his teeth at Tommy, coated with bits of cake and cream but still square and whole and tooth-shaped.

Tommy weighed the meringue in his hand, marvelling at its feather lightness. He took a small bite and held the sugary morsel in his mouth, letting it dissolve very very slowly against his teeth.

A sharp elbow dug his ribs. 'Tommy!' Frankie's dismayed voice hissed in his ear. 'It's Miss Hattersley!'

Tommy's heart sank,. They weren't supposed to eat in the streets; it was one of the strictest of school rules and now, striding towards them was not just a teacher, but the headmistress herself. Any moment she would see them. Of all the rotten luck!

'We saw Miss Hattersley talking to you,' said Jenny when they were in the boat. 'What did she want?'

'Oh, nothing,' said Tommy. 'She was just talking.'

'Your face was all red. What had you been up to?'

'Nothing,' Tommy snapped. 'And mind your own business

anyway!'

When they reached the island they met Mrs Scarrot on her way back from the hen house. Her arms were splattered with dirt and straw was caught in her hair.

'You'll have to do something about that hen!' she told Mr Scarrot. 'Look at the state of me, and I still haven't collected the eggs!'

Mr Scarrot sighed. 'Doris again, is it?'

They all went down to the hen house and stared at the cause of all the trouble. Doris, one of the older hens, had become broody and for the past week had insisted on gathering all the eggs in the nesting box beneath her, billowing down upon them with a flouncing of feathers like a crinoline and sitting on them for hours. Getting the eggs from beneath her had become a daily battle. Mr Scarrot had tried a cluster of china eggs but after the first time Doris had not been taken in. She clung to the real eggs with grim determination, sharp beak ready to peck anyone who dared to put a hand near them.

'We should re-christen her Miss Jean Broody,' said Poppy.

'Why?' demanded Tommy.

Poppy did not deign to answer.

'Come on, Alice,' said Mr Scarrot. 'I'll move Doris and you grab the eggs.'

He bent down and pushed at the broody hen. She squawked indignantly and pushed back but he managed to dislodge her long enough for Mrs Scarrot to snatch a handful of eggs.

'Why does she do it?' asked Jenny as they walked back to the house.

'She wants to raise a family,' Mr Scarrot explained. 'She thinks if she sits on them long enough they'll hatch into chicks.'

'Poor thing. Can't we let her hatch a few?'

Now Jenny, you know eggs won't turn into chicks unless you've got a cockerel,' said Mr Scarrot. 'She could sit on them for ten weeks and they'd still be eggs and in the meantime she's not laying and she's stopping us collecting. No, there's only one thing for it. She'll have to go into solitary.'

'But that's not fair! Just because she wants to start a family. I bet you didn't put Mam in solitary when she wanted to have us!

Mr Scarrot laughed at Jenny's indignant face. 'That was a bit different.'

If anyone asked Mrs Scarrot what was her favourite occupation she would answer without hesitation. Cooking. There were many other things she enjoyed, such as playing the piano, growing roses, tucking Charlie into bed at night, polishing her mahogany dining table until it shone, picking blackberries, or sitting over an early morning cup of tea and making lists of what she would buy if she had a thousand pounds. But cooking was the thing she liked best to do.

The thing she liked least to do was the weekly wash. In fact, she would go so far as to say she hated it. Sometimes she woke in the night from nightmares of steaming white shirts, dripping blue jeans and baskets of dirty grey socks; and in the morning her first waking thought was not, what time is it? or, is the sun shining? but, is it washday? And if it was, she would pull the sheet over her head and mutter that one of these days she would go on strike, yes, she would. And then what would they all do?

If only she had a washing machine, she moaned. But you couldn't have a washing machine without electricity, Mr Scarrot had answered reasonably, and bringing electricity to a small island in the middle of a lake would cost a fortune.

'Couldn't we have our own electricity? A windmill? A generator?'

A thoughtful gleam had lit Mr Scarrot's eyes and he had promised to consider the possibility. That was a year ago and he was still considering it, occasionally in the evenings bringing out a drawing pad and making neat careful diagrams which he coloured in pretty pastel colours with Jenny's box of crayons.

Without a washing machine the weekly wash occupied almost the whole of Saturday, starting at half past six in the morning. Mrs Scarrot had never dared to count how many shirts, sheets, dresses or other large items she washed each week, but once she had counted the socks and stockings and there had been twenty one pairs of white socks, thirty five pairs of grey and navy plus one odd black, and twenty three pairs of nylon tights. Having a family of eleven was all very well but on washdays she could do without them.

At least, she told herself as she filled a zinc tub with boiling water and put the dirtiest clothes to soak, at least she didn't have anything else to do on that day of the week. Aunt Mabel and Grandma cooked the dinner, Poppy and Jenny did the sweeping and dusting, and the others washed dishes and brought her cups of tea or cool drinks, depending on whether she was cold and disgruntled or hot and flustered. But she would far rather have done all those things herself if only someone would, just once, offer to do the weekly wash.

With a sigh she shook out a rolled up sock. That was another thing. No one ever turned their dirty clothes right side out or unrolled their socks or emptied their pockets ready for the wash. Pockets were the worst. The things she had found in people's pockets! With a shudder she remembered the roll of pound notes that had gone unnoticed into the boiling tub with Mr Scarrot's white overall one ill-fated Saturday last summer. Payment for a whole van load of vegetables. She had watched the shreds floating up through the suds. But it made no difference, he still forgot to empty his pockets.

Cross, she picked up his brown check trousers and extracted five screws, a drawing pin, two packets of seeds, a bottle of rooting compound, a Chewy Mint and a lipstick. A lipstick? Mrs Scarrot unwrapped the mint and popped it into her mouth while she considered the shiny gilt tube. Red Romance, it said on the bottom.

Aunt Mabel's shining blonde head appeared around the washhouse door. Cautiously, because Mrs Scarrot on washdays was not the Mrs Scarrot that the family knew during the rest of the week. On washdays she was a dancing bear with corns, a monkey with a sore tail, a crocodile with toothache.

'Alice, dear,' whispered Aunt Mabel. 'Alice, dear, so sorry to bother you, but have you found my lipstick? Fred said he picked it up in the van and he thinks he put it in his pocket.'

Without comment Mrs Scarrot handed it to her, dislodged the mint with difficulty from her back teeth and laid it on the the window sill beside Mr Scarrot's screws.

Jack's best grey trousers were in the wash again. Now *they* shouldn't be dirty, she'd washed them only last week and she was sure he'd only worn them once since then. She fished out two guitar plectrums, a folded up photograph of Elvis Presley and a tin of Fisherman's Friend throat tablets, then laid the trousers aside. She would do them if there was time.

The pile of retrieved objects on the window sill grew higher. A paperback book of crosswords - Mrs Scarrot put it aside to look at between rinsings - two buttons and a drawing of her best friend Karen from Jenny's school blazer; a hearing aid battery from Grandma's blue striped dress; one of Aunt Mabel's false eyelashes; Uncle Arthur's pocket book of birds; 10p and a handkerchief from Poppy's tennis shorts.

And from Tommy's grey trouser pocket ...

'A-a-ah! Ugh! *Tommy*!'

Mrs Scarrot's shriek brought not only Tommy but the whole household stampeding into the washhouse, where Alice stood like Lady Macbeth, staring at hands covered, not in blood, but in a thick glutinous mess that pulled in sinister threads between her spread fingers.

'Tommy!' Her voice was deep as doom. 'What is this?'

Tommy lowered his eyes to the floor and shuffled.

'It's meringue,' he whispered. 'Frankie Filkin bought me one yesterday, and then Miss Hattersley came along and I stuffed it in my pocket quick. And - and I forgot it.'

Mrs Scarrot slumped against the sink. 'Tommy Scarrot, you'll be the death of me. Go and fetch me a knife.'

Tommy blanched. 'A - a knife?'

'A knife.'

The others had gone when Tommy returned. He handed the knife to Mrs Scarrot. She turned his pocket inside out and began to scrape the mess on to a newspaper.

He waited in silence for a moment, then, 'Can I have it?' he asked.

'Have it? What for?'

'To eat.'

Mrs Scarrot stared at the remains of the meringue, melted and grey with pocket fluff, stuck with bits of grass and what looked like an ant.

'No, you may not.' She finished scraping and with a final shudder wrapped the paper over the mess.

'You may carry that to the dustbin,' she said. 'No opening it again, mind. You're to put it straight into the dustbin. Promise?'

'Promise,' said Tommy. (I'll put the *newspaper* straight into the bin, he qualified to himself).

He carried the bundle out of the washhouse, shutting the door with a kick of his foot behind him.

Seven paces brought him to the dustbin. Before he reached it, he had managed to insert one hand into the newspaper, scoop up the meringue and stuff it into his mouth, pocket fluff, grass, ant and all.

10

The Carnival

It was tea time. Tommy was hungry, having missed both the meat and potato pie and the pork sausages at school by being on third sitting. Although he had eaten the chopped ham salad that the dinner lady had offered him instead, it was not what he considered to be proper food, not for a boy, anyway.

After helping himself to a spoonful of his mother's plum chutney and two spoonfuls of Piccallilli (which, being shop bought and not home made, was far more of a treat) and two tomatoes, he lifted the lid off the cheese dish and cut a large wedge of Cheddar. Feeling his mother's watchful eye on his bent head, he concealed the wedge beneath a slice of bread and, to distract her attention, announced:

'There's to be a carnival on the 27th September.'

'Tommy, that's too much cheese. We've no more until I go to the shops on Friday.'

'There's going to be floats,' added Jenny. 'Our school's doing Hansel and Gretel in the Gingerbread House.'

'Tommy, that's enough!'

With an air of injury Tommy replaced the further thin slice he had pared off the cheese. 'I was just tidying it.'

'Yes, well, seeing it untidy doesn't bother me at all,' said Mrs Scarrot.

'Anyone can enter,' said Jenny. 'The Boy Scouts are doing a

spaceship and Mr Carter's doing pigs.'

Mr Scarrot looked up from his plate. 'Pigs?'

'Real pigs?' asked Tommy.

'I don't know,' Jenny mumbled through a mouthful of fruit cake.

'But why pigs?'

'He's a butcher,' said Mr Scarrot. 'It's a good advertisement for him.' Thoughtful now, he spread butter on a slice of bread and added Marmite. 'What's it in aid of?'

Jenny shrugged. 'Don't know. The church roof, I think.'

Jack came in. 'Roll on the end of term!' he said, pulling out his chair with a gusty sigh.

'But you've only just started,' said Mrs Scarrot.

'I know, but I think old Fowler is feeling the strain already. He's set us three hours extra homework just because Johnny Stiles thought Disraeli was the leader of the Blackshirts in Italy.' He buttered four slices of bread and lifted the cheese dish lid. 'Who's eaten all the cheese?'

'Tommy.'

Tommy glared at his mother indignantly. 'I did not. I only ate half of it.'

'Wonder if Ben Jackson would let me borrow his flatbed truck,' mused Mr Scarrot.

Mrs Scarrot looked at him. 'What are you thinking of now, Fred?'

'Entering the carnival. We could have a banner - Fred Scarrot' Vegetables - Fresh from Pineapple Island. It's good business, advertising.'

Tommy jumped up and down. 'Oh yes, Dad, let's. We can all sit on the float!'

'We could all dress up as vegetables,' Jenny giggled. 'I'll be a - a cabbage, and Tommy, you can be a beetroot - and Grandma can be a cauliflower ... '

'And Jack can be a potato. One of those big lumpy ones with eyes in it,' said Tommy. Jack kicked him under the table.

'Poppy,' called Jenny as her elder sister came through the door.

'You can be a stick of celery.'

'What?'

And little Charlie can be a Dwarf French Bean,' suggested Jack.

Tommy snorted, blowing out cheesy crumbs across the table. Charlie, hearing his name, looked up from his bowl of Shredded Wheat with hot milk and bestowed a wide impartial smile of delight on his family.

'Aunt Mabel can be a big yellow pumpkin,' said Mrs Scarrot, joining in the fun.

'What about Uncle Arthur?'

'A marrow.' Jenny giggled again. 'What about you, Mam?'

Mrs Scarrot preened. 'Oh, I shall wear my purple dress and be an aubergine.'

Tommy snorteds again and the others dodged the crumbs. Mr Scarrot leaned forward, his eyes alight.,

'We'll do it!'

'Do what?'

'What you've just said. I'll drive the truck and you can all be vegetables. Fred Scarrot's Vegetables!'

Tommy broke the silence. 'But - But Dad. We were only joking.'

Mr Scarrot smiled at the dismayed faces around him. 'Ah, sometimes it doesn't pay to joke. Sometimes it gives other people ideas!'

'But Fred, it's ridiculous,' Mrs Scarrot protested later that evening. 'Besides, it's only the end of next week. I couldn't sew costumes in such a short time. And think of the expense - all that material for eleven people.'

'Ten. I'll be driving.'

'Perhaps Mr Jackson won't lend you the lorry,' said Grampa.

'He owes me one or two favours. I don't think he'll refuse.'

'I'm not going to do it,' Jack burst out. 'I'm not going to dress up as a vegetable! All my friends will laugh at me - and what if someone hears about it when I'm famous. It would be all over the newspapers that Jackie Quicksilver once drove through Kenmere as a potato! Oh, they'd love that!'

'Well, I think it's a wonderful idea,' said Aunt Mabel. 'No one's going to laugh at you, Jack, and anyway, it's only a bit of fun, isn't it? Who knows, we might even win first prize.'

'And pigs might fly,' said Grandma.

'Well, I don't mind,' said Poppy. 'As long as I can be something pretty. What d'you think, Dad?'

Mr Scarrot looked at her fondly. 'You'd make a lovely young lettuce, love. All fresh and green and delicate.'

Poppy's round cheeks grew pink with pleasure and Jack made a noise like someone being sick.

'Crepe paper,' said Tommy.

They stared at him.

'We use it in school for headdresses and things. You remember when we did the Folk Dances of the World, Mam?' All the caps and bonnets were made of crepe paper.'

'And the flower garlands in the hall,' added Jenny.

'I suppose we could try,' Mrs Scarrot said slowly. 'But I hope someone else has some ideas on how to do it - because I certainly haven't!'

The dining room was set aside as a workshop, and soon it was festooned with rolls of crepe paper in every shade. Mr Scarrot bought a stapling gun, three boxes of staples, two rolls of sticky tape and a new measuring tape for Mrs Scarrot after she had found her old one glued to Tommy's door with a thick red line alongside the 47 inch mark.

Aunt Mabel took over the role of chief designer and decided to make cloaks of green crepe paper to represent stems. Above these the Scarrots would wear large headdresses, each representing a different vegetable.

'We'll have to use clips and hat pins to keep them on,' she said.

'Good job we won't have to dance about,' muttered Mrs Scarrot. 'It's all a bit precarious, if you ask me.' She consulted her list. 'Charlie next. But how on earth would you make a Dwarf French Bean?'

Aunt Mabel considered. 'Hmmm, not so easy. A bean hasn't really any outstanding characteristics, has it?'

'You could do a cluster,' suggested Poppy. 'Hanging around his face.'

'Good idea, Poppy. Now, what have we got so far? Cauliflower for Grandma - I'm pleased with that one, it's turned out well. Cabbage for Uncle Arthur, lettuce for Poppy, French bean for Charlie. It's all green, isn't it? We need some bright colours.'

'What about sweetcorn? A nice bright yellow?' Mrs Scarrot suggested.

'Can't have sweetcorn,' said Mr Scarrot who had popped his head around the door to check on progress.

'Why not?'

'I don't grow it.'

'Does that matter?'

It's an advertisement for my vegetables, isn't it? And if I don't grow them I can't advertise them, can I? Wouldn't be honest.'

'Well, start growing it then.'

'Can't. Tried before. It just won't grow for me.'

Mrs Scarrot sighed. 'Sometimes you do make life difficult, Fred.'

By the night of the 25th the costumes were completed, the drapes and banners prepared for the lorry and the dining room restored to its normal purpose.

'We should have a dress rehearsal,' said Aunt Mabel.

'Tomorrow,' said Mrs Scarrot with a weary sigh. 'After breakfast tomorrow.'

'I'm not going to do it!' Jack's voice was shrill. 'A potato was bad enough but now you've made me a carrot!' His face, framed by a feathery frill of green beneath a bright orange cone, was red with rage. Poppy bit her lip and turned away, trying to hide her laughter.

'Neither am I!' Tommy moved to stand beside his brother and began to wrestle with his purple beetroot headdress. It was anchored to his head with clips and elastic bands and there was an ominous ripping sound.

'Don't you tear that costume! Mrs Scarrot warned. She stared at herself in the mirror and pushed her aubergine headress to a more rakish angle. 'They're right, you know, Fred. We do look silly. I'm not going to do it either.'

'Nonsense,' said Mr Scarrot. 'You'll all look marvellous once you're on the truck with green baize and crepe paper grass all around you and my banners flying in the breeze.'

'It's all very well for you. You're driving. No one will see you.' She looked at the others. 'I say we vote on it. Hands up all those who don't want to do it.'

Three hands shot into the air: Jack's, Tommy's and Mrs Scarrot's. They were followed more slowly by those of Grandma, Grampa, Uncle Arthur and Jenny.

Mr Scarrot stared at Aunt Mabel. 'What about you, Mabel? You're not going to desert me as well, are you?'

'I'm sorry, Fred, but it's a democratic vote. I'll have to go with the majority.' Her hand rose.

Last was Poppy. Secretly she was rather taken with herself in her lettuce costume. The bright green leaves that haloed her head did something for her, she felt. Gave her round face a certain piquancy. She raised her hand with reluctance, wondering as she did so if any of the other floats might by any chance be able to use a lettuce.

'That's it, then!' Mrs Scarrot was triumphant.

'You've forgotten Charlie,' said Mr Scarrot.

'He doesn't count, he's below voting age.' Mrs Scarrot gave her husband a pitying smile. 'It's no good, dear, you've lost. You might as well give in gracefully. We're not going to do it.'

But eleven o'clock on the morning of the Carnival found the Scarrots huddling amongst the green baize billows of Mr Jackson's decorated lorry, which Mr Scarrot was edging towards the starting point of the parade.

'Keep in front of me, you two,' Jack hissed at Poppy and Jenny. 'If anyone sees me I'll kill myself!'

'I think you look quite sweet,' whispered Poppy.

'Shut up!'

Mrs Scarrot, trying to pretend she was there merely to look after the children, flashed quick glances at the floats nearest to her. Why, there's Mrs Castleton, she said to herself, at once feeling much better about the whole thing. For that lady, fifty if she was a day and all of thirteen stone, was bedecked in black tights, a black and orange striped leotard and a black furry cap upon which two long black antenna quivered in the breeze. She was perched atop a large model of a beehive, surrounded by a dozen smaller bees, children from the junior school, but Mrs Castleton swelled above them all, a smiling Queen Bee, caring not a jot that her orange and black stripes bulged in places that a bee never bulged.

Mrs Scarrot turned to her family. 'Come on, everyone,' she jollied them. Let's look as if we're enjoying ourselves. Wave to the crowds!'

Jack stared at her with disgust. 'Traitor!' he muttered.

The procession started off and began its tour of the town. There were few holidaymakers so late in the season but news of the Carnival had brought visitors from all the villages nearby and from Keswick, Penrith and even Lancaster. Two-way traffic was halted in the centre of the town as the lorries and cars manoeuvred through some of the narrower streets and crowds thronged the pavements,

Jenny and Tommy began to feel good, high above the upturned faces. They felt quite superior to those who were taking no part in the parade. Amongst the crowds Poppy noticed Steven Bateman, the best looking boy in her class. He was looking up at her with a grin of appreciation, and gave her a thumbs up. Blushing but delighted, she fluttered her lettuce leaves at him. The only one who wished he wasn't there was Jack, who squeezed his eyes tight shut when he saw two girls from his class nudge each other and giggle as the Scarrot's float drove by

It was a cool day, cloudy, and the Scarrots wore their ordinary clothes beneath their green cloaks, but soon they began to shiver as the small early breeze strengthened and set the banners flapping. The breeze brought more clouds, small, grey and white edged, and then a larger one, thick and slate coloured, that spread its wide low canopy over the procession.

Plop!

Mrs Scarrot stared at the drop of rain that was forming a dark circle on the bright emerald green of her cloak.

Plop, plop! There were murmurs from below and the crowds retreated into the shelter of shop doorways.

Mrs Scarrot turned to the cab of the lorry and banged on the back window. When Mr Scarrot glanced over his shoulder she mouthed words at him and jerked her finger upwards at the sky. Turning back to the wheel he peered through the windscreen, then shrugged his shoulders. There was nothing he could do. There was no turning back. At least eight floats were strung out behind them and in front were another five.

The rain quickened to a relentless downpour but there was no escape for the line of floats. On they drove, at seven miles an hour as the crowds of onlookers dwindled to a determined few.

Tommy's cloak gave way first. He watched in wonder as the expanse of sodden green crepe paper across his lap split, exposing a pair of green-stained knees. He lifted his hand and saw that the palm was also bright green.

A drooping lettuce leaf curled forward and plastered itself across Poppy's left eye. She shivered, and as Jack's bright orange carrot cone crumpled into a shapeless mound on top of his head he swore vengeance on his father, Tommy and the whole world.

'Hey, Fred, your vegetables are wilting!' called a wit from the pavement.

Mr Scarrot ignored him, more concerned with how he could avoid the wrath of his family when this endless procession was over.

It did at last come to an end, but by then the Scarrot family were a sorry sight. Others had suffered but none quite so totally. The Mayor and Mayoress were judging the floats, and Mrs Scarrot turned pink with embarrassment when she saw them peer, baffled, at the Scarrot float and turn to the organisers for whispered explanations,.

The infant school won first prize. Mrs Hansard, the art teacher, had *not* used crepe paper, and the Gingerbread House was resplendent and unharmed, with Hansel, Gretel and the Witch waving, dry and triumphant, through its windows. The Boy Scouts, singing camping songs around a very realistic painted wooden bonfire, came second and Mrs Castleton's beehive came third.

When the judging was over the Mayor cleared his throat.

'Er ... there is one final prize. A small one, but no less important. This is the prize for Effort and I think in the circumstances - ' He looked up at the sky - 'my wife and I are agreed that this - er - should be awarded to Mr Scarrot for his - er - vegetable float, which is - er - um - might have been - um ... Mr Scarrot, would you step forward, please?'

There was silence in the Scarrot van as they returned to Kenmere. Silence as they paddled the raft across to Pineapple Island. Silence as they trooped into the house and separated to wash and change into dry clothing.

Mr Scarrot hurried to the kitchen, stoked up the stove and filled the kettle. A nice cup of hot tea might, he hoped, pacify his family.

He almost dropped the kettle on his foot when a loud wail emerged from Poppy's bedroom.

'It won't come off!'

Within seconds the whole family had invaded the kitchen. Mr Scarrot stared aghast as they advanced on him, their faces, hands and arms stained and streaked with green, yellow, red and purple dye. He backed towards the door.

'At least we won a prize,' he pleaded.

'Booby prize!' Mrs Scarrot's voice was cold.

'It - it'll come off eventually,' he stammered. 'Won't it?'

'How should I know?' she snapped. 'I'm not in the habit of wearing crepe paper in the rain.'

Tommy kept very quiet. It had after all been his idea.

'Well, there's one blessing,' said Aunt Mabel, turning away from the kitchen mirror with a shudder. 'At least we live on an island. I vote we tie the boat up and hibernate for a week!'

Mr Scarrot took his cup of tea to the farthest corner of the kitchen and tried to make himself invisible. He averted his eyes from his multi-coloured family. It would be a long time before they forgave him.

Belatedly he remembered the small wrapped parcel with which the Mayor had presented him and which he had shoved into his trouser pocket. Drawing it forth he tore open the wrapping and stared at the slim book within. The title was 'Modelling With Paper'.

11

The Competition

In the Scarrot household it was not unusual to pick up a packet of cornflakes or soap powder or sultanas and find its contents trickling out of a neatly removed square of cardboard, or to start an interesting article in a newspaper or magazine, only to discover when turning to page ten as instructed that its final paragraphs had been marked with ten crosses on the reverse and posted off to London or Edinburgh.

Many a time Jenny, who was the culprit, had been grateful that her family were not the sort of persons who fly into insane rages, jump up and down and throw teacups at the wall when such things happen (although she would not have blamed them if they had, for she had to agree it must be very frustrating). Just the same, it was nice that they were so patient, because she would carry on doing it anyway. For, just as her father could not resist auctions, Jenny could not resist competitions. A great deal of her time and most of her pocket money was spent in cutting out and posting away competition entries. Any competition. She didn't mind if she had to colour a picture of a starship, choose the six most important features of a washing machine (even though the Scarrots didn't have one) or circle an invisible football. Some competitions were more interesting than others, and some had more exciting prizes, but it made little difference. If it was a competition Jenny entered it. And that was that.

She had entered over a hundred competitions since she started and won only one prize, a £2 voucher for garden compost. But she was not daunted. Someday - quite soon, she was sure - she would win again and then it would be something really splendid. (You have to be an optimist if you enter competitions.)

One day, after Mr Scarrot had at last installed a generator, there was great excitement when he brought home from a sale a small television set. For the first time the family were able to enjoy the wonders of the small screen.

For a time Mrs Scarrot and Poppy became passionately involved in the tangled and tortuous lives of the residents of Coronation Street, and although Mrs Scarrot never actually hurried the family through tea, she did get fidgety if the table had not been cleared and the dishes washed by half past seven. Jack watched Top of the Pops with strained attention, hoping for a glimpse of his idol, Elvis Presley; Tommy and Jenny quarrelled each afternoon over the choice of children's programmes, and Mr Scarrot dropped all his tools, neglected his vegetable plots and watched everything.

It didn't last. The novelty wore off and much to the relief of Grandma and Grampa and Uncle Arthur and Aunt Mabel, who were used to television and couldn't see what all the excitement was about, the family settled down to their normal lives again. Jack still made an occasional random check of the music programmes for Elvis Presley and Mr Scarrot made a point of watching Gardeners' World, but most of the time the set languished on a shelf in the sitting room, covered by a lace mat carrying a porcelain lady in a yellow crinoline.

Jenny, however, remained devoted to one children's programme. It was a new programme called Blue Peter, and she became quite fierce in defence of her right to crouch before the little television set twice a week and be greeted by those popular figures Leila and Christopher. She liked the animals that always appeared in the studio: dogs and cats, and others more exotic, like the elephant, and the large python that slithered around Leila's neck during the whole of one programme. And she liked all the things they taught you how to make. Useful things for Mothers Day and Christmas and birthdays.

One day Blue Peter announced a competition. Jenny was delighted. Moreover, when she heard what the competition was to be she felt a rising flutter of excitement.

'This is it,' she thought. 'I'm going to win at last!'

There was no doubt in her mind. For Blue Peter wanted their

viewers to write essays about their homes, and the best and most interesting would win a Major Prize. The prize was something so exciting that the producers of Blue Peter had decided it would remain a mystery until the actual presentation. Jenny had a moment's curiosity about the prize but she didn't mind waiting. She knew it was hers, there was no question of it. For who had a better or more interesting home than Jenny?

She flew to her bedroom for an exercise book and her best pencil. So full of enthusiasm was she that the words flooded from her mind faster than her pencil could write them. It took her an hour to write the essay and when she had finished she thought it was the best thing she had ever done. She put it away until the following morning, read it through, altered a word her and there, then copied it out on pale blue crinkle-edged paper in her best handwriting.

Although she sometimes told her family about the competitions she entered, this time she wanted to keep it to herself and she slipped the thick blue envelope into her coat pocket to post at the letter box near her school.

After the entry had been posted she tried to put the competition out of her mind but it was not easy. Confident as she was, she couldn't help the odd sneaking doubts that assail people when they want something badly. What if her entry was lost? At school they had seen a film about the Post Office, and remembering the thousands and thousands of letters that were collected, sorted at sorting offices, bagged, sent off in trains and re-sorted, it seemed to Jenny that it would be very easy to lose one small pale blue envelope.

And what if - the thought brought her bolt upright in bed one night - what if there just happened to be someone, one person, who had a home more interesting than hers? Perhaps someone lived in a circus or - or a lighthouse. Would that be more interesting? No, no, of course it wouldn't, she reassured herself, and she lay back and closed her eyes again.

It was six weeks later that the letter came. The postman always left the Scarrot's post at Colonel Fitzbudgett's house, and on that particular Saturday morning Mr Scarrot called and collected four long brown envelopes, the kind that had little transparent windows over the addresses and contained demands for money, a gaudy bundle of advertising circulars and a large important-looking white envelope with a line of thick black lettering across the top.

'One for you here, Jenny,' said Mr Scarrot. 'The BBC! What have you been up to?'

Jenny stared at the envelope. It was addressed to her. Miss Jennifer Scarrot, Pineapple Island, Lake Kenmere, Cumbria. She tried to bring her hand forward to take it but she was trembling so much that all she could do was to stare at the thick black lettering until it swam before her eyes.

'You open it for me, Dad,' she whispered at last, and then she closed her eyes and listened to the rustle of paper and the sudden intake of Mr Scarrot's breath.

'Jenny!' She heard her father's voice as if from a great distance. 'You've won a Major Prize!'

Soon the entire household was gathered in the sitting room and Mr Scarrot was pouring glasses of his rhubarb wine for everyone, even a tiny drop for Charlie.

Jenny was hugged and kissed and looked at with new respect.

'I knew I'd win,' she kept saying. 'No one else has a home like mine!'

'But that's only half of it,' Mrs Scarrot said. 'You must have written a good essay, dear, and spelled all the words properly.'

'Oh, that was nothing,' said Jenny, and believed it. Anyone, she thought, could have written a good essay about Pineapple Island. It was such a wonderful place that the essay almost wrote itself.

Later Jenny took the Blue Peter letter to her bedroom and read it again quietly. It was signed by Leila and Christopher and it invited her to the Blue Peter studio to appear on the programme and receive her prize. With the letter were four return rail tickets, for herself, her parents and one other member of her family.

Jenny let the letter drop to her knee and stared at the rail tickets, feeling excitement rush through her like bubbly lemonade. In two weeks she would be in London!

In two weeks she would be on television!

12

Cats and Robbers

Tell us a story, Aunt Mabel!'

Aunt Mabel laughed and closed her book. 'All right. Choose something from the chest.'

Tommy lunged forward and Jenny's voice rose. 'Hey, I asked first!'

'But it's my turn,' said Tommy.

'No, it's not, it was your turn on Tuesday.'

'Children, children! If you're going to squabble, we won't have a story at all. Jenny, you choose.'

Jenny peered into the chest, her hand hovering over the treasures within. She reached down and picked out a tiny red velvet collar with a gold medallion.

'This, Aunt Mabel.'

'Let me see.' Aunt Mabel took the collar, unbuckled it and stretched it out along the top of the chest. 'That was Yorky's,' she said. There was a soft smile on her face as she played with the small medallion.

'When we go to London,' she said at last, 'I'll show you the pub your Uncle Arthur and I used to have. A lovely place it is, real Victorian, with glossy green tiles, shining mahogany counters, brass handles everywhere, and those big mirrors engraved all over with leaves and flowers. And we kept it real nice, didn't we, Arthur?'

Uncle Arthur opened his eyes and nodded.

'We always had plenty of customers and at lunchtimes I used to serve hot snacks - baked potatoes filled with hot bubbling cheese, or sour cream and chives, or hot chopped bacon and peppers, and toasted sandwiches, and sausages in batter.'

Tommy licked his lips.

'We used to get all the theatre crowd, the actors and the singers and the dancers. And Thursdays and Saturdays we got the market people. Have you ever seen a street market?' Aunt Mabel asked Tommy and Jenny.

'No, never.'

She laughed. 'There's nothing like a London street market. Stall after stall after stall of everything you can imagine. Fruit and vegetables piled up, scarlet, green and yellow. Shoes and plastic buckets and lace shawls, and bright pink soap and miracle chrome cleaners. Wigs and china shepherdesses and brass candlesticks and dolls' houses!

'And the people - West Indian, Italian, Pakistani, French, Chinese, African - every race and colour you could think of, they all come on Thursdays and Saturdays'.

She rebuckled the little collar and dangled it over her finger.

'Our cat, Yorky, liked to see all the people. He was a Brown Burmese cat, you know, a lovely glossy chocolate colour - that's why we called him Yorky, after the chocolate bars.'

The children smiled.

'He liked to wander into the bar and sit on the counter where he could be noticed. Burmese cats like company, you know. They like to sit on your shoulder and nuzzle their little noses into your neck and talk to you. Lovely and friendly, Burmese are,' she said with a sigh, her face saddening.

'Well, one night - it was a Thursday, wasn't it, Arthur?' Uncle Arthur nodded. 'One night we'd just got the last customer out and locked the doors and we were about to start on all the washing up and wiping down - we always did it there and then, not like some who'd leave it a mess until morning - when there came a tremendous knocking on the side door. "Who's that?" I asked, for we never had anyone knocking after we'd closed for the night. "Police," a voice said. "Sergeant Cribley." Well, we never thought anything of it, even though the voice was a bit muffled, because we knew Sergeant Cribley, quite a regular he was. "There's been an accident," he said, and all of a flutter, of course, I rushed to unlock the door ... '

Tommy found he was hardly breathing. 'And what happened, Aunt Mabel?'

'As I opened the door, a huge figure pushed past me. He slammed and relocked the door and turned to face us. And it was *not* Sergeant Cribley!'

Jenny gasped and gripped the wooden arm of her chair.

'We couldn't see his face, for he had a nylon stocking pulled down over it, which flattened his nose and stretched his eyes and pulled his lips into a hideous shape, and he breathed with a strange hissing sound.'

'Oh, Aunt Mabel!'

'Your Uncle Arthur and I were trembling with fear, and there was nothing we could do, for he had a small black evil-looking gun trained on us. He waved it towards the till and said "Get me the takings!" Well, there was a lot of money in the till, hundreds of pounds, but what could I do? If we didn't give it to him he might shoot us, so with heavy hearts your Uncle Arthur and I took out the money and tied it up in bags and tossed it to the floor by his feet as he ordered. And then ... '

Jenny's and Tommy's eyes widened. 'And then -?'

'Then Yorky sauntered into the bar and leapt up on to the counter. And then - you'll never believe what happened next. The robber started to shake. He shook and he shook, and his gun wobbled backwards and forwards, and he began to back towards the door, forgetting all about the money at his feet. And Yorky, being a friendly cat, jumped down from the counter and followed him, purring all the while.'

Jenny stared at her. 'I don't understand. What was wrong with the robber?'

'He was frightened. Frightened of Yorky!'

'That's silly,' said Tommy. 'Fancy being frightened of a cat.'

'But lots of people are frightened of cats,' said Aunt Mabel. 'Terrified, in fact. Just as people are often terrified of snakes or spiders or the dark. It's called a 'phobia', and when people are frightened they can't always control what they do.'

'Is that why you have Yorky's collar?' Jenny asked in a small voice. 'Did the robber shoot him?'

'Not at all,' said Aunt Mabel. 'All of a sudden Yorky made a tremendous leap right up on to the robber's shoulder, and that terrified him so much that he dropped his gun, scrabbled at the door and rushed off into the night without either his gun *or* the money.'

'What happened then, Aunt Mabel?'

'We rushed to phone the police and they caught him. And then the next day we bought that little gold medallion and had it engraved for Yorky.'

Jenny picked up the collar and scrutinised the medallion.

'What does it say?' asked Tommy.

Jenny read out the tiny inscribed words: 'To Yorky, for bravery in the face of the enemy' on one side, and on the other: 'From his grateful owners, Arthur and Mabel Scarrot.'

She handed the collar and medallion back to Aunt Mabel, who replaced it in the chest and closed the lid.

'Where's Yorky now?' Jenny dared to ask at last.

Aunt Mabel sighed. 'He died a week later. He was run over, right outside the pub . Your Uncle Arthur and I swore we'd never have another cat.'

There was silence.

'*We've* never had a cat,' Tommy said after a while.

'A cat couldn't get run over on the island,' said Jenny, after a further long pause.

Aunt Mabel smiled. 'Hmmm. That's true enough.'

13

To London

It was the day of the Blue Peter presentation.

All the family wanted to see Jenny receive her prize, and after much discussion and argument it had been agreed that they would all go to London, and hang the expense! Jenny had written to Blue Peter asking for ten seats for the show, Mrs Scarrot had bought a new dress for Jenny and a hat for herself, and now they were off, whirling through England towards the Capital on a fast train.

'Look at Charlie,' Aunt Mabel laughed. Charlie's small curly head was swinging from side to side as he tried to follow the scenery that rushed past the windows.

'He'll be sick,' warned Grandma.

'Here, Charlie, play with this.' From her large shiny black handbag Mrs Scarrot produced the snowstorm paperweight which she had snatched up at the last minute from the hall table. Entranced, Charlie turned the paperweight up and down, shook it, licked it, and went off to sleep with it clutched to his chest.

Aunt Mabel leaned back in her seat. 'We'll show you our pub before we go to the studio. And the market will be on today, seeing it's Wednesday.'

It was many years since the children had visited London. Jenny and Tommy had been so young that they remembered nothing, and their arrival at Euston Station was an unnerving experience. They were bewildered by the milling, pushing crowds who shouted in a dozen different languages, the strangled announcements that blared out over the loudspeakers, the swift hum of the electric trolleys that sent them leaping out of the way, and the hisses of the trains as they entered and left the huge busy station.

Outside in the streets it was worse. It was raining, great gusts of rain that lashed at their faces like wet sheets. Umbrellas spiked them as the damp heedless crowds rushed past, and the traffic snarled bumper to bumper along the wet roads, headlights flickering through the rain.

Jenny's heart sank. She didn't think she was going to like London. It was wet and noisy, it smelled funny, there were too many people, and no one said Sorry when they bumped you.

When the family descended into the bowels of the earth to catch a Tube train she liked it even less and for a moment almost wished that they could turn tail and catch a train straight back to their green and peaceful Cumbria.

But when they left the Underground at Stratford they found that the rain had ceased, the pavements shone like liquid gold and, although the crowds still bunped you, they smiled and said 'Sorry, Ducks,' when they did so.

Aunt Mabel, despite her varicose veins, developed a spring in her walk.

'Come on, children, it's just round the corner!'

And there it was. A jewel of a place, sparkling green tiles below, sparkling etched glass above, and a bright swinging sign that pictured a white-wigged gentleman in a scarlet coat and white breeches.

'He looks like my soldier,' said Tommy.

'That's the Duke of Argyle,' Aunt Mabel told him.

Inside the pub the bright slanting rays of the sun caught glittering mirrors and polished wood, swirled through drifts of cigarette smoke and shone alike on seamed old faces and rosy young ones. A rich smell of steak and onions lay on the air.

A loud shriek pierced the room. 'Mabel! Arthur!'

From behind the counter bustled a fat woman with red cheeks, silver hoop earrings and a frizzed halo of black hair.

'Mabel! Whatever are you doing back here?'

'Hello, Annie. It's lovely to see you again.'

The two women embraced, and Aunt Mabel's high-rise curls tilted sideways, losing a couple of hair grips in the process. 'Where's Albert?'

As she spoke, a pink polished head with two strands of mouse brown hair glued across its top appeared from somewhere beneath the counter. It belonged to a tiny man carrying a large crate of beer bottles.

'Albert, look who's here!'

There followed more embraces, slaps on backs and excited explanations. Uncle Arthur was still silent but his smile stretched from ear to ear.

Soon the Scarrots were seated around a large mahogany table. Before them were plates of hot steaming food, with tankards of beer for the men, sherry for the ladies and lemonade for the children.

'Well,' said Aunt Mabel. 'What d'you think of our pub? A bit of all right, isn't it?'

Tommy looked around him. 'It's lovely, Aunt Mabel. And the food's smashing.'

'Hmmm. Not *quite* as good as mine, but good enough.'

Later Aunt Mabel and Uncle Arthur took the family on a trip through the colourful street market. It was a very quick trip, for they were due at the television studio in less than an hour, but there was just time to buy a poster of Elvis Presley for Jack, an Indian silk scarf for Poppy and a brilliant pink plush teddy bear for Charlie.

Then, after a last minute panic because they had missed the Tube train, they were at the studio and the family, still flushed and breathless, found themselves separated from Jenny and seated in a row of chairs facing the familiar set of Blue Peter. Jenny, looking pale and scared, had been whisked away through a heavy steel door.

Soon the well known signature tune was playing and the popular figures of Leila and Christopher appeared, to be greeted by a loud cheer from the younger members of the audience.

The programme was half way through when at last Jenny was announced. The Scarrots saw her appear off set, a small figure picking her way across the trailing cables of the cameras and lights. A young woman hovered beside her, peering at her face through large hornrimmed spectacles and making sudden dabs at her nose with a powder puff.

Christopher was talking into one of the cameras, explaining the competition and showing the viewers the huge sacks containing thousands upon thousands of essays. 'And believe me, we at Blue Peter have read every one!' he said with a rueful laugh. 'And now we would like to introduce to you the young lady who wrote what we all considered to be the best and most interesting essay of them all - Miss Jennifer Scarrot!'

Mrs Scarrot leaned forward, clutching her handbag, as Christopher took Jenny's elbow and led her to a seat beside his. Mr Scarrot rubbed damp hands between his knees, and Grandma over-adjusted her hearing aid and had to turn it back when it screeched.

Then Christopher was talking about the major prize.

'We kept it a secret because we feel that this is one of the best prizes we have ever offered and we feel sure that Jenny and her parents will be excited when they learn just what Jenny has won.'

He paused and the audience held its breath.

'To make the announcement I would like to call on Mr Henry Tulley of Stellar Travel Limited.'

Mr and Mrs Scarrot held their breath as Mr Tulley appeared, bearing a large white envelope. Mr Tulley himself was rather small and looked ill at ease under the bright lights and unblinking eyes of the television cameras. Sweat was already breaking through the powder that the horn rimmed lady had puffed over his face, and he ran a finger round the inside of his collar as if it were suddenly too tight for him.

He seemed to have some difficulty in opening the envelope, dropping it twice in his struggles, but at last it was done and he pulled out a large gilt-edged card.

'Miss Scarrot,' he said, turning to Jenny. 'On behalf of Blue Peter, in conjunction with Stellar Travel Limited, I would like to present you with this voucher, which entitles you and your family to an eight day holiday, all expenses paid, in the beautiful city of Venice, Italy, the holiday to be taken at any date between February 8th and May 5th next year!'

Venice! There was a gasp of delight from the Scarrot family and the rest of the audience.

'Well, Jenny?' Leila and Christopher were smiling broadly.'What do you think of your prize?'

'It's - it's - I can't believe it!' Jenny stammered, but during the next few moments as Blue Peter showed picture after picture of the beautiful buildings and canals of Venice she found her mouth stretching in an uncontrollable smile.

'Now then,' said Christopher as the pictures came to an end. 'Before we ask you to read your prizewinning essay, I would like to stress that this very special holiday is for your *whole* family, and therefore, so we can let Mr Tulley go away and prepare all the forms and documents, perhaps we can ask you, Jenny, to tell us how many you have in your family.'

'Well,' said Jenny, settling herself into her chair. 'There's my Mam and Dad ... '

Christopher smiled and nodded encouragement.

'And my big brother Jack ... '

She waited as Mr Tulley wrote down the names in a large green file.

'And Poppy and Tommy ... '

Christopher's smile began to falter, and Mr Tulley's head lifted from his file.

'And Charlie - he's the youngest ... '

She paused again as Mr Tulley cleared his throat.

'And Grandma and Grampa, and Uncle Arthur and Aunt Mabel - Oh, and me, of course!' she finished happily.

Christopher loosened his grip on the arms of his chair and gave Jenny a weak smile.

'Well - er - Jenny, that's quite a large family, isn't it? I - er - I make that eleven in all. Is that right?"

'Yes, that's right. There they are, over there.' Jenny pointed to the audience. A camera swung towards the Scarrot family and Mrs Scarrot adjusted her new white hat.

A helpless look passed between Christopher and Mr Tulley, whose face had turned quite pale.

.'Er - Jenny ... Christopher shifted in his chair. 'Actually, by family we meant *immediate* family, if you see what I mean.'

'Immediate?' Jenny repeated, not understanding.

'Parents. Brothers and sisters.'

'But - but we couldn't leave Grandma and Grampa behind, they're too old to row the boat or the raft!'

'No, no, of course not,' Christopher muttered.

'And Aunt Mabel's got her varicose veins!'

Aunt Mabel flushed and tucked her legs beneath her seat.

'Er - Jenny, would you excuse us a moment?'

Leila rushed forward and began to demonstrate how to make a merry-go-round from two cream cheese boxes and a pair of knitting needles, while

Christopher ushered Mr Tulley off the set.

When Leila had finished, the two men returned and seated themselves on either side of Jenny. The camera swung towards them and they both forced broad smiles to their faces.

'Well, Jenny, I now have an announcement to make. The producers of Blue Peter and the directors of Stellar Travel Limited have with great generosity agreed to make a special concession, and I am therefore very pleased to announce that the WHOLE SCARROT FAMILY will go to Venice next Spring - all ELEVEN of them!' He smiled a further sickly smile into the camera. 'And now I will ask Miss Jennifer Scarrot to read to us the essay which has won for ALL ELEVEN MEMBERS of the Scarrot family this fabulous prize!'

Jenny gave her family a triumphant grin, crossed her legs, smoothed her new blue spotted dress over her knees and picked up her essay.

'If I could choose to live anywhere in the whole wide world,' she began, 'I would still choose Pineapple Island ... .'

14

Bakers to the Rescue

The weather was damp and murky when they emerged into the streets of London. Although still only half past four, dusk was creeping down the long wet pavements, and after the brightness and glitter of the studios everything appeared dull and dreary and depressing, the way it often does when you've climbed a high peak of excitement and then found there's nothing else for it when you've reached the top but to slide down again.

The Scarrots hovered outside the studios, not knowing quite what they wanted to do but reluctant to descend into the Underground and catch the Tube to Euston.

The home-going crowds hurried along, parting and rejoining around the clustered figures like waves around a rock, and a sudden surging babel of sound caught their attention as a young policeman sauntered past, his two way radio in his hand.

'Wait here!' said Mr Scarrot and then he was running after the uniformed figure.

'What's he doing?' asked Grandma.

'Don't know,' said Mrs Scarrot. 'Maybe he's going to ask the time.'

But when Mr Scarrot returned he was smiling.

'We're going to have a slap-up tea,' he announced. 'Finish the day off with a bang. There's a good Italian place around the corner, the bobby says.'

'Oh, Fred,' said Mrs Scarrot. 'Can we afford it?'

'What about the train?' asked Grampa.

'We'll catch the next one. There's always plenty of trains from London.'

The restaurant was called Capaldis. and a rosy welcoming light spilled out from its windows. A hand written menu card hung beside a poster of Naples and promised unfamiliar delights.

'I won't have to eat anything with eggs in it, will I?' asked Tommy.

'Of course not,' said Poppy. 'It's all tomatoes and peppers and things, isn't it, Mam?'

But Mrs Scarrot was not listening. She was staring into the window of the shop next door.

'Fred, couldn't we have our photo taken? All together, a proper portrait? We've never had a picture of the whole family before, it would be a nice souvenir of the occasion.'

The shop was a photographic studio and its window was filled with portraits of bridal couples and angelic golden haired children. No prices were on display but Mr Scarrot was filled with a devil-may-care, hang-the-expense elation, and within seconds they had all crowded inside and the photographer, a tall stooped man with faded blue eyes and a drooping moustache, was attempting to squeeze them into the very small space that fronted a dusty potted palm and even dustier green velvet drapes.

'You'll have to come in a little closer, Madam,' he said to Aunt Mabel.

'I'm already standing on someone's toes. Oh, it's you, dear.' Aunt Mabel smiled into Uncle Arthur's pained face. 'Why ever didn't you say something?' She removed her offending foot and allowed it to hover in mid-air.

Poppy tried to move backwards, overbalanced and caught the velvet drape, releasing a thick cloud of dust. Grampa produced a gigantic sneeze, almost losing his false teeth. Charlie seized the moment to announce that he wanted to pee-pee, not later, *now*!

But at last, after much shuffling and rearrangement, the photographer was able to confine them all within the frame of his viewfinder.

'Now, everyone, breathe in and smile, please. A nice big smile.'

The Scarrot obeyed, there was a long frozen moment that seemed to go on forever and then it was done.

'You'll have it within the week, Sir,' promised the photographer as he squeezed them through th door and out into the stdreet.

'Good job we hadn't already eaten,' said Aunt Mabel. 'He'd never have got us all in together!'

The waiter at Capaldi's greeted them with upflung hands, rolling eyes and a flood of Italian when he saw the size of their party, and his Mama who sat on a dais behind an enormous brass cash till had mild hysterics, but once they had pushed three tables together all was quiet again. Soon they were tucking into plates of pasta heaped with thick spicy meat and tomato sauce.

Jenny watched an olive skinned boy at a nearby table twirl spaghetti around the prongs of his fork and slip it with perfect efficiency into his mouth. She copied him and was just about to bite on the large ball of spaghetti when it sprang from her fork and slid down her chin and on to her lap.

Aunt Mabel laughed. 'I should leave that for the experts, love. Much safer to cut it up with a knife and fork.'

The pasta was followed by flat glass dishes of Neapolitan ice cream, pink, green and white, and coffee in tiny black cups.

Thirty minutes later they were on the Underground train to Euston.

'That was a lovely idea of yours, Fred.' Grampa patted his warm full stomach. 'I reckon I might have a nice little nap on the way home,' he said, his eyes already closing.

Mr Scarrot had not been mistaken when he said there were plenty of trains from London. There were. Unfortunately they were not all bound for the North, and the Scarrots had to wait more than an hour at Euston before at last they were on their way. Mr Scarrot had also failed to consider that when they arrived at Preston there might not be a connection to take them on the last lap of their journey. In fact, when they reached Preston, much later than expected, they found that the last train had departed more than an hour ago.

'But what are we to do?' Mrs Scarrot gazed at the station master in dismay.

'It's not British Rail's fault, Madam. There's not much I can do in the circumstances. However, if you can't afford a taxi or a hotel for the night, I could offer you the station waiting room. There's a train at 7.45 tomorrow morning. I've a couple of blankets you can have for Grannie there and the little ones.'

There was nothing else to do. Taking the two blankets, and eleven cardboard cups of weak tea from a vending machine, the Scarrot settled themselves in the bleak waiting room to wait for morning.

It was a dreadful night. Even the children woke several times, cold and stiff on the narrow benches. Each time Mr Scarrot opened his eyes and peered at his watch it was to find that no more than ten or fifteen minutes had crawled by.

At three o'clock he woke to find Jack shaking his shoulder.

'Dad! Dad, I've found a super place to spend the rest of the night!' he hissed. 'They said we can all go round there, and they'll fix up some cushions and blankets for us. It's a great place, Dad, all warm and smelly!'

'But - ' Mr Scarrot groped for understanding. 'Where've you been?'

'I couldn't sleep. I went for a walk and I found it, just around the corner. It's a bakery, Dad. A bakery, and they're going to give us tea and hot bread. Come on, hurry, let's wake the others.'

The sight of the Scarrot family, pale, dazed, wrinkled and cold, would have aroused sympathy in the hardest heart. The bakers were a kindly lot, and in no time at all mugs of strong hot tea and plates of hot floury rolls were being pressed upon the weary family. Soon they were glowing in the wonderful heat from the huge ovens and sure that no food had ever tasted quite so wonderful as that before them.

Afterwards, with a promise to wake them at twenty minutes past seven, the men left the family to sleep in a quiet corner of the bakery, and even Mr Scarrot's eyes remained closed until he was awakened again by a friendly hand on his shoulder and another cup of tea.

I feel as if we've been away for a week,' said Mrs Scarrot when at ten o'clock that morning they arrived back at Pineapple Island. She gazed around her at the familiar sights of home. It had been raining in Cumbria too, and water dripped from the trees to the soft brown earth, but a shaft of sunlight was piercing the clouds. She thought of the noise and bustle of London and decided that, glad though she had been to go, she was ever, *ever*, so glad to come home again.

'I'm sorry I messed things up last night,' said Mr Scarrot.

'That's all right, Fred. It was no one's fault. It was a new experience, anyway.'

'It was an adventure!' said Jack. 'We all did things we've never done before.'

'Dad,' Tommy pulled his father's sleeve. 'How many exams do you have to pass to be a baker?'

Mr Scarrot smiled. 'Oh, lots and lots, I should think. You'd better start studying as soon as you go back to school!'

15

Christmas Is Coming!

Christmas drew nearer and nearer. It was time for the children to retreat to their rooms with glue and paper, cloth and cardboard, hang KEEP OUT or KNOCK BEFORE ENTERING signs on their doors, and behind them frown and mutter, tear up, screw up, throw away and restart their gifts. It was a time when brains, ingenuity and nimble fingers were more important than money - for there was never enough money to buy presents for so many.

Tommy was ahead of everyone else. He had made three gifts already. He was rather proud of Aunt Mabel's, which was a felt covered matchbox in which to keep her eyelashes. On the end he had glued a blue silk tassel which had fallen off the fringe of his bedspread. Well, it hadn't *completely* fallen off, but it was very loose. For Grandma he had made a calendar with a crayonned picture on each page of one of the Scarrot family. Tommy himself was on Page One, of course, January; and as there were only eleven Scarrots he hadn't bothered to make a page for December. He didn't suppose Grandma would notice. Most calendars got lost before December anyway.

His present for his mother brought an occasional twinge of anxiety. He was growing an orange tree from a pip, but each time he dug it up for inspection it looked the same as before. Well, there were still nineteen days to Christmas. Perhaps it was too late to expect oranges, but at least it should have some leaves by then.

Like Tommy, Jenny had started with Aunt Mabel's present.

Somehow it was easy to think of gifts for Aunt Mabel, and Jenny had made her a necklace like the one she had worn in an old photograph of her dancing days. It had meant a big sacrifice for Jenny, for she too had her little drawer of souvenirs and one of her most precious was a beautiful scarlet silk poppy brought back by Mr Scarrot from a Service of Remembrance he had attended five years ago. Jenny had hesitated for a long time before sewing it to a narrow black velvet ribbon, with poppers to fasten, and it was only the thought of how splendid it would look against Aunt Mabel's golden hair and white neck that stopped her from taking it straight off again.

Charlie was still too young to care or worry about Christmas and the problems of gift-giving, yet somehow he sensed the excitement and the preparations, and his enthusiasm to join in and be at the centre of whatever was happening caused many a calamity. KEEP OUT notices meant nothing to him and the others' anguished cries of 'Oh Charlie, go away!' did nothing to halt his relentless advance.

One place where Charlie was NOT ALLOWED was Mr Scarrot's workshop.

'Far too dangerous for a little imp like Charlie,' Mr Scarrot announced when he bought the big steel padlock to secure its door. Mrs Scarrot agreed. The thought of all those sharp knives and saws and drills in Charlie's eager hands made her shudder and she was glad that no one in the family other than Mr Scarrot was interested in using the workshop. The longer it was locked up the better, as far as she was concerned.

That December, however, as Jack pondered on the problem of providing ten gifts with less than £1, he had a sudden inspiration. Bookends! At the back of the workshop there was a huge pile of wood offcuts. He just had to choose the right sizes, sandpaper them smooth, then glue and nail them together and he would have presents suitable for all the family. Why, everyone had books. Even Charlie had two, although his were made of rag and he preferred to suck rather than read them.

'Mind you lock up after yourself,' warned Mr Scarrot when Jack asked his permission to use the workshop.

Soon a KEEP OUT sign appeared on the door, and from inside came a banging and a hammering that aroused even Grandma's curiosity, who as Christmas drew near kept her hearing aid switched on more and more, so that she would miss no clues as to who was giving what to whom.

The banging and sawing went on for two days, with an occasional howl as Jack forgot he was resting his voice and burst into song - although the first time he did so Mrs Scarrot, who had also forgotten just how disconcerting Jack's voice could be, rushed into the workshop with lint and bandages, expecting a dreadful accident.

Then silence descended, and Jack emerged with a large box, draped in an old sheet, and staggered in the direction of his bedroom. A few moments later he returned, retrieved his KEEP OUT notice and pinned it to his bedroom door, giving Tommy and Jenny a stern look as they hovered outside.

'What d'you think he's made?' whispered Jenny. 'It's an awfully big box.'

'I don't know,' Tommy whispered back, 'but I hope it's for me. I like big presents.'

Over breakfast each morning the children compared progress.

'How many have *you* made?' they asked each other, and, 'I can't think what to make for Uncle Arthur!' and, 'Can you lend me some glue/paper/green wool/red felt/black ink?'

Jack leaned back in his chair the morning after his two day sojourn in the workshop and gave them a patronising smile.

'I've finished all mine.'

The others looked at each other.

'Did you make them all in the workshop?' Jenny asked.

Jack hesitated, then nodded.

'Are they all made of wood?' Poppy fished.

Tommy clapped his hands. 'Twenty Questions! Jack has to answer Yes or No and - '

Jack stood up. 'No, no more clues. You'll just have to wait for

Christmas Day.'

Later that morning Mrs Scarrot looked up from the marzipan that she was kneading for the Christmas cake. She stared around the big empty kitchen, aware that something was bothering her, had been bothering her for the last half hour or so. She frowned, with a vague feeling that something was wrong. Then she realised what it was. It was too quiet.

She listened. She could hear Jenny picking out a tune on the piano, and she could hear the amiable squabbling of Grampa and Grandma as they enjoyed a game of Scrabble in the sitting room. Outside she could hear the faraway clucking of the chickens as they were shooed into the hen house so that Jack could dig over the run. But amongst the many small noises of home one was missing. Long moments passed before she realised what it was. It was the sound of Charlie. The constant droning chatter that accompanied most of his waking hours as he practised his newest words. The noise ceased only when Charlie was either asleep or doing something very naughty, and Mrs Scarrot knew he couldn't be asleep because it was only two hours since breakfast.

She sighed and called Jenny.

'Charlie's up to mischief somewhere. Will you look around the house and let me know what he's doing?'

When Jenny returned , she was followed by Poppy and Tommy.

'He's not in the house.'

'But he must be. He can't open the front or back doors himself and no one's been outside since your Dad and Jack, and Charlie was still in the bath then.'

Poppy's hand flew to her mouth. 'I fetched some logs from the woodpile after breakfast. Perhaps he slipped out then.'

Mrs Scarrot put a damp tea towel over the marzipan. 'Well, get your coats on, all of you. We'll have to search for him. Heaven knows what he might be up to by now!'

But when they gathered together again some quarter of an hour later, Charlie had still not been found and their faces showed their worry as they stared at each other. It was far worse than when Grandma had gone missing, for after all Grandma was older and sensible - or usually so - but Charlie could be doing all sorts of dreadful things and could have hurt himself or - or worse.

Except for Mr Scarrot, who was delivering vegetables in Keswick, the whole family now assembled in the kitchen. Mrs Scarrot took out her handkerchief and screwed it between her fingers, pushing away thoughts of the lake. All the children had been trained to keep away from the water's edge until they could swim. Even Charlie wouldn't ... She tore a small hole in the handkerchief.

'We - we'll have to be systematic,' she said. 'We'll split up, each take one section of the island, and Tommy, you look through the house again - and don't forget the cupboards, you know what he's like.' (With sudden hope she lifted the lid of the bread bin that stood on the kitchen floor, but Charlie was not there. Really, he was too big now to climb inside.)

'Well, off you go. The first one to find him - ' Her voice trembled. 'Whistle for the rest of us.'

All over the island voices could be heard calling for Charlie, but no answer came. The cries became more and more despondent.

Jack searched the stream and its banks. Tommy and Jenny had built a little bridge out of old wood, and if Charlie ... Jack stopped in his tracks. Wood! No one would have thought to search the workshop, for it was always kept padlocked, but ... Had he locked it last night when he finished? *Had he?* A sudden terribl vision filled his eyes. Sharp glittering tools, razor sharp as Mr Scarrot liked to keep them. Blood. And Charlie. He began to run.

'It's no good,' said Poppy, having beaten her way though the branches of the old laurel thicket and come face to face with Uncle Arthur. 'He just isn't anywhere.'

Uncle Arthur nodded. They stared at each other in despair.

Then the whistle came. Poppy's eyes widened. 'They've found him. Quick, they've found him!'

Mrs Scarrot and Grampa were the first to reach the workshop. Jack stood at the door, his face pale. 'I'm sorry, Mam. It's all my fault. I forgot to lock up.'

Mrs Scarrot's face whitened and she pushed past him. Behind her the others craned to look over her shoulder.

'What - what is it?' Jenny whispered.

'It's Charlie,' Jack replied.

But - but that's not Charlie, thought Jenny. That *can't* be Charlie.

What she and the others saw was a strange sawdust covered lump. Odd growths sprouted from its surface, and it squatted, shapeless, mute and unmoving, on the floor at the rear of the workshop beneath the silent horrified gaze of the Scarrots.

'Charlie?' Mrs Scarrot whispered.

And then at the centre of the lump the growths began to stir. They became recognisable as clumps of wood shavings and as they stirred some fell away, disclosing two small glittering eyes from which trickled two disconsolate streams of tears. A small wail was heard and Mrs Scarrot rushed forward.

'Oh Charlie! My poor little boy!' She tried to pick him up,.

'Oh, Charlie!'

He was glued to the floor.

It took three hours to clean off the wood shavings, sawdust and glue, and it was a very sore and red skinned little boy who fell into an exhausted sleep that afternoon. Jack had some explaining to do when Mr Scarrot returned and learned what had happened.

'Fancy leaving the door unlocked,' he scolded.

'I'm sorry, Dad.' Jack's voice faltered. 'It won't happen again.'

'It certainly won't. You won't be using my workshop again!'

Jack agreed. At that moment he was sure he would never ever want to. He also had a feeling that it would be a long long time before Charlie was tempted to explore its attractions again!

16

Christmas

Gifts made, concealed within mysterious wrappings and hidden at the backs of cupboards and under beds, the children were now free to join in with the other preparations for Christmas. The plum pudding had long been made, complete with secret wishes and a stir of Mrs Scarrot's big wooden spoon, but there were other goodies to prepare.

Jenny and Tommy, under Aunt Mabel's supervision, made coconut ice and peppermint creams, Jack boiled a large pan of treacle toffee, and from Mrs Scarrot's left over marzipan Poppy fashioned the most beautiful fruits - apples, oranges, strawberries and bananas - which she coloured and set out in frilled white paper cases. Grandma made her special rich brandy-soaked mincemeat and Mr Scarrot, Grampa and Uncle Arthur had a trial testing of the barley wine that Mr Scarrot had made and bottled three years ago, which was now good enough to paste silly smiles on their faces.

Charlie ... Well, Charlie just made a mess.

It was a lovely time, quite the best time of the year. The house filled with spicy smells, log fires roared and crackled up the big stone chimney, baskets of chestnuts stood in the hearth ready for roasting, and outside skies were dark and a fine powdery snow was falling. Soon Mr Scarrot would uproot a fir tree to stand in the hall.

There were so many things to do. Holly and mistletoe to gather and wire into scarlet braided wreaths; paper chains to cut out and glue; cards to address; the tree to decorate; windows to frost and hang with cut out stars; the beautiful nativity figures that had belonged to Grandma's own mother to unwrap and set out in the straw crib; and through all the flurry and activity that wonderful sense of excitement and anticipation.

There was nothing, *nothing,* quite like Christmas!

But there was something else to look forward to. Jenny was organising a Grand Concert on the evening of Christmas Day. It was an idea that had sprung fully formed into her mind on the night of Jack's concert earlier in the year. Why shouldn't the whole family give one, each doing a song or a dance or a recital in turn? It would be such fun, and what better time to have it than on Christmas Day?

Full of enthusiasm she had tackled the family and found some equally enthusiastic but others a little nervous.

'Ooh, I couldn't do anything,' said Grandma. 'I've never been on a stage in my life! No, no, I couldn't do anything.'

'But Grandma, it will be just us,' Jenny pleaded. 'And *we* won't mind how terrible you are.'

'Terrible?' Grandma bristled. 'Who said I'd be terrible? If the others can do it, then so can I!'

Jenny meant to excuse Uncle Arthur. After all, what could he do when he wouldn't speak? But Aunt Mabel wouldn't hear of it.

'Oh, my Arthur will come up with something,' she said with a mysterious smile.

Soon Jenny had a promise from everyone, except Charlie, of course - and she even had something planned for him.

She decided that each item on the programme should be a surprise, but this caused problems as the one place to rehearse in secret was the soundproofed music room. It was not long before squabbles developed and Mr Scarrot had to step in and arrange a rota so that each person had their allotted time to rehearse.

On the afternoon of Christmas Eve Mrs Scarrot put her foot down.

'No more rehearsing! It's Christmas Eve and I don't want to hear another word about the concert until 7 o'clock tomorrow night. Now then,' she continued with a grim smile, 'there's ten pounds of potatoes to peel, three pounds of Brussels sprouts, four pounds of carrots and three pounds of parsnips - and the stuffing to mix. Who's going to help?'

On Christmas Day the Scarrots awoke to a transformed silent world. A thick white blanket of the purest softest snow shimmered and sparkled beneath a blue, blue sky and the snow-hung trees were like giant glittering puffballs. It was a sight to take your breath away.

Later the children would rush outside to roll in the snow and bombard each other with snowballs, but now there were more important things to concern them, such as Christmas stockings filled with nuts and chocolate pennies and fruit and tiny silly toys. And later still, after breakfast in front of the glowing red kitchen stove, there would be the exchange of presents.

'Happy Christmas, everyone!' Hugs and kisses and warm loving arms and chocolate-smeared embraces. Hot platters of bacon and egg on the big pine table, and the tantalising smell of roasting turkey already drifting from the oven.

'I've finished, Mam,' said Tommy after one bite of his buttered toast. 'Can we give our presents now?'

'No, Tommy, not yet. First we have to wash the dishes and tidy the house, and then we'll take a walk,' Mrs Scarrot teased. She laughed at his downcast face. 'Ten minutes,' she promised.

And ten minutes later all the family assembled in the hall around the Christmas tree. The presents had been brought out of hiding and stacked beneath it, and now, as at every Christmas before, each person could receive one present in turn, to be opened, exclaimed over and admired before the next person opened theirs. It was a slow process and Tommy found the suspense almost unbearable, but that was the way it had always been done.

Charlie, being youngest, was first, and the first present that Mrs Scarrot selected for him chanced to be Jack's bookends. Charlie, after examining and tasting the wrapping paper, tore it off and inspected the bookends with interest. A smile lit his face. He picked them up and banged them together.

'Clappers!' said Tommy. 'What a good idea, Jack.'

'Well, actually - '

'I'm next, Mam!' Tommy bounced up and down on his heels as Mrs Scarrot chose a large flat package for him. It was from Mr Scarrot.

'O-o-oh!' Tommy exclaimed with delight when he uncovered a beautiful hand made bow and a quiver of feathered arrows.

'Not to be used when anyone else is within range,' warned his father. 'And no shooting at birds!'

Jenny's first present from Aunt Mabel and Uncle Arthur puzzled her. It was a soft foam filled cushion, covered in crimson velvet, but an unusual shape, like a round plate with a six inch wall surrounding it. She looked a question at Aunt Mabel.

'That's half your present,' Aunt Mabel said. 'You'll understand when you get the other half.'

With relief, for she had to admit she had felt just the tiniest bit disappointed, Jenny laid the cushion beside her and watched as the others opened their gifts. She liked the frilled and beribboned petticoat Aunt Mabel gave Poppy, and Mr Scarrot's wine rack from Uncle Arthur, and Grampa's new pipe, whose bowl was carved into the head of a Red Indian. She admired Jack's music stand and the spice cupboard filled with tiny labelled drawers that Mr Scarrot had made for Mrs Scarrot, and the big book on birds that Grandma and Grampa gave Uncle Arthur. She smiled when Grandma stared at her bookends from Jack, murmering 'Clappers?' and she stared anxiously as Mrs Scarrot opened Tommy's present and peered at the small pot of wet soil inside.

'It's all right, Mam.' Tommy snatched the pot from her and gouged out the pip with his finger. 'Look, it's got a little nobble on it now,' he said, pointing out the tiny protuberance. 'It'll be a tree soon!'

The purpose of Jack's bookends became clear as more were opened, and Jack lost his sheepish expression as the family congratulated him on his handiwork.

Soon the floor was a gaudy sea of wrapping paper and tinsel, and after two hours all the presents had been opened. Jenny could see that Tommy was also disappointed with his present from Aunt Mabel and Uncle Arthur, which was a set of three yellow dishes that stacked on top of each other, and she wondered at the purpose of such strange presents. Besides, Aunt Mabel had said that was only half of it. Where was the other half?

Then Uncle Arthur, who had disappeared a few minutes before, came back with a large square box. It was an ordinary brown cardboard box, but a scarlet ribbon had been tied round it.

Aunt Mabel spoke. 'I told Jenny and Tommy that half their present was still to come. Here it is, children, and a very happy Christmas!'"

The two children rose and stepped forward. Jenny reached out a hand and touched the box. Six small holes had been punched in the lid, and from inside came a small scuffling noise. And then the cushion and the dishes had meaning.

The others fell silent as they watched, and in that silence the sound that came from the box was small but very clear.

'Mia-ao-uw!'

Jenny and Tommy stared at each other, mouths falling open. They touched the box with trembling fingers.

'Well?' said Aunt Mabel. 'Aren't you going to open it?'

17

The Concert

Year after year Mrs Scarrot's Christmas Dinner proved to her family that she was the absolute best, the absolutely finest cook in the world. It was always a jolly occasion, with crackers and paper hats and candles, and it was the one meal of the year when everyone tucked in with enthusiasm, knowing that no one would accuse them of being greedy. After all, who could resist thick white slices of turkey with crisply browned edges, garnished with tiny sausages and bacon rolls? Or golden-roasted potatoes and hot buttered vegetables? Or Mrs Scarrot's plum pudding made from her own secret recipe and aflame with brandy? Or her sizzling hot mince pies smothered with whipped cream? Or her home made chocolate and rum truffles?

But on this Christmas Day Tommy and Jenny did not do perfect justice to the tempting meal which was placed before them. The reason lay beneath Mrs Scarrot's best white damask tablecloth, first on one lap and then on the other: the tiny Burmese kitten, the other half of Tommy's and Jenny's present from Aunt Mabel and Uncle Arthur. By general agreement he had been named Cadbury, in honour of his beautiful milk chocolate coloured coat, and the children had spent all afternoon playing with him. They had even taken him outside into the soft white snow, although this had not been completely successful. Cadbury, after testing the snow with one dainty paw, voiced a firm protest in his strange deep miaow.

With a smile Mrs Scarrot noticed Jenny's hand reaching yet again beneath the table to stroke the kitten.

'You haven't forgotten you're in charge of the concert after dinner?' she reminded her.

Jenny in her excitement had indeed forgotten.

'I'll look after Cadbury,' Tommy rushed to offer.

Jenny hesitated, reluctant to give up the kitten for a whole evening, but the concert had been her idea and - as Miss Hattersley, their school headmistress, had once said: people, even boys and girls, must never evade their responsibilities.

Thus, after dinner was finished and the family had washed, dried and put away the dozens of dishes which had been used, Jenny went to the sitting room, where the concert was to be held.

Jack and Poppy had offered to move the furniture, as Jenny was too small, but the organisation was to be all hers. She had decided to arrange the chairs facing away from the window, so that those performing could enter through the door from the hall. Mr Scarrot had put a line across the room at ceiling level, from which had been hung makeshift curtains (the remainder of Mrs Scarrot's peony patterned material) to divide off the stage area, and across the wall behind them the children had pinned length after length of home made paper chains in scarlet and blue. At either side of the piano they placed Mrs Scarrot's two tall rubber plants, strewn with gold and silver tinsel. When they had finished they all agreed that the stage looked as good as any theatre in the land.

Then Jenny produced her programme, which she had printed in thick black letters on a large card, and pinned it to the wall in front of the stage curtains so that all the audience could read it. There were nine acts on the programme. Jenny herself would appear twice, once with Charlie and once with Tommy, for neither of them, she felt, was old enough to perform alone.

Mrs Scarrot was Number One on the programme, and an hour later the rest of the family took their seats facing the stage and waited for her to appear. But first Jenny rose and stood in front of the curtains, a hand raised for silence. In a loud clear voice she read from the speech she had prepared the night before.

'Ladies and Gentlemen,' she said. 'This is the first concert by the whole Scarrot family and I hope everyone is going to enjoy it. It's called a Grand Mystery Concert because all the acts are secret, but I hope you're going to clap them all even if they're awful! After all, it *is* Christmas. The first act is my Mam, and she's the only one that's not secret, because we couldn't hide the piano. Ladies and Gentlemen - Mrs Alice Scarrot!'

Jack and Mr Scarrot jumped up to open the curtains, revealing Mrs Scarrot seated at the piano in her best navy blue satin dress, which was a little bit tighter than it had been the Christmas before,. Nevertheless she looked very pretty, and so did the piano, for she had put candles in the two silver sconces and on the top stood a bowl of holly and ivy.

With her foot on the loud pedal she burst into a spirited medley from the musical Oliver! and the audience settled back into its seats to enjoy the concert.

Jenny was glad she had decided to put her mother on first, for everyone liked music and the long loud applause that followed gave her time to grab Charlie and rush him out of the room to get changed. Even so they were both breathless when they returned and she waved a hand through the gap in the curtains as a signal to her father to open them.

The audience gave a murmur of appreciation when they saw Jenny in the long plain white robe she had made from an old sheet, fastened with her blue dressing gown cord. Charlie wore a soldier's uniform contrived from a pair of dark blue dungarees, a scarlet jersey, two white crepe bandages crossed over his chest and a navy blue cap from Tommy's Post Office game. Around his neck hung a scarlet and white tin drum.

Jenny began to sing. It was The Little Drummer Boy. The audience quietened as they listened to her small clear voice. Charlie, of course, was the Drummer Boy himself but for the first half of Jenny's song he was more interested in investigating an ancient toffee which he had found in the pocket of his dungarees and to which the paper wrapper had become welded. At last, abandoning all attempts to unwrap it and popping it into his mouth just as it was, he suddenly remembered that he should be performing. Thenceforth the act was all Charlie's as he grabbed his drumsticks and began an enthusiastic tattoo on his drum that drowned Jenny's little voice. The audience decided at this point to clap and Jenny, giving the whole thing up as a bad job, led Charlie on a march round and round the stage, which he enjoyed so much she had to carry him off.

She had a chance to relax as Grampa and Mr Scarrot performed a very competent tap dance, wearing home made top hats, black bow ties and old fashioned patent leather tap shoes that Mr Scarrot had found at a sale. His shoes were very tight so that he found it hard to keep his smile after a few minutes, and Grampa soon began to puff and stagger, but the audience thought they were wonderful.

'Grampa always did like Fred Astaire,' said Grandma. 'Saw all his films five or six times, he did.'

Poppy was next. Dressed in a long black skirt and frilled white blouse, her hair shining in the lamplight, she sang three songs, accompanied on the piano by Mrs Scarrot. Her voice was pure and true, and when she had finished there was a storm of clapping, everyone agreeing that she was much better than Julie Andrews.

Then it was time for Jenny and Tommy. But Tommy, after Jenny had hurried him into the hall, stood his ground with a mutinous expression on his face.

'I'm not going to do that stupid Dutch dance.'

'Don't be silly, you've got to. It's all rehearsed and they're waiting for us!'

'I'm not going to. I feel daft tippy-toeing about in those stupid baggy trousers.'

Jenny stared at him in dismay. There were times when Tommy made up his mind and no one could budge him. She could see that this was one of them.

'But you've got to do something. Everyone has.'

'I am going to do something. I'm going to recite a poem.'

Of course. Why hadn't Jenny thought of that? Tommy had one unusual talent. If something interested him he could read it half a dozen times and then remember it in complete detail. She had heard Mr Scarrot call it a 'photographic memory.'

'All right,' she said. 'Have you got to get changed?'

'No. I just need to fetch something from my bedroom.'

'Well, *hurry up*!'

She slipped back into the room.

'Ladies and Gentlemen. We're sorry to keep you waiting, but there's been a small change in the programme. Tommy Scarrot, Act Five, will now perform by himself.'

When Tommy appeared he was still dressed in his thick yellow pullover and brown cord trousers, but on his head was the new Red Indian headress that Grandma and Grampa had given him for Christmas, four bright streaks of blue and red chalk decorated his cheeks and he carried the bow and arrow his father had made for him. Walking to the centre of the stage, he closed his eyes and began to recite.

Downward through the evening twilight
In the days that are forgotten
In the unremembered ages
From the full moon fell Nokomis ...

Ah! Everyone remembered Longfellow's famous poem. Even Grandma and Grampa had learned it when they went to school. Mr Scarrot gave Tommy an approving smile. He liked a touch of the classics.

See! a star falls! said the people,
There among the ferns and mosses ...

Grampa found himself nodding as the regular insistent rhythm of the words washed over him and combined with the effects of that second helping of pudding he had been unable to resist. He jerked his head up. Mustn't let Tommy see him dozing off.

By the shores of Gitche Gumee,
By the shining Big-Sea-Water ...

THE FAMILY ON PINEAPPLE ISLAND

Jenny began to feel uneasy. Just how much of the poem did Tommy remember? He couldn't know it all! Last year it had taken her class two whole lessons to do Hiawatha!

Then he said to Hiawatha:
Go, my son, into the forest
Where the red deer herd together ...

Tommy went on and on. And on. And on. Jack began to bite his nails, while the others shifted in their seats.

Made a cloak for Hiawatha
From the red deer's flesh Nokomis
Made a banquet in his honour ...

Jenny tried to recall how many more verses were still to come. But she had none of Tommy's talent for remembering such things.

Called him Strong Heart, Soan-ge-taha!
Called him Loon Heart, Mahn-go-taysee!

Perhaps if she pretended to faint, Jenny thought, he would stop. But then they might send her to bed and she'd miss the rest of the concert.

At last Tommy came to the end. By that time Grandma had turned off her hearing aid, Grampa was asleep and the rest of the family were so numb that it was a moment before they realised he had finished. Then the relief was so great that their applause was loud enough to shake the house. Delighted, Tommy offered an encore but Mr Scarrot said Thank you very much but it wouldn't leave time for the others.

The family had now watched five acts of the Grand Mystery Concert, and after Tommy's epic poem Mrs Scarrot decided it was time for an interval. They all rose, stretching their stiff legs and massaging the pins and needles out of their posteriors.

'A nice cup of tea and a hot mince pie, that's what we need,' she said.

They moved to the big warm kitchen, and Mrs Scarrot and Aunt Mabel made tea in two huge brown teapots while the older children took the plates of mince pies from the stove and set out bowls of thick cream to accompany them. On the pine table, beneath folded white napkins, were plates of turkey and ham sandwiches, dishes of chutney and pickles, winter salads, chocolate truffles and Christmas cake. Tommy couldn't see them but he knew they were there. Reciting made you awfully hungry, he realised, and wondered if his mother would let him have just one turkey sandwich. But the covered food was for supper after the concert and he knew she would say no.

18

The Concert - Part Two

After the family returned to their seats four Acts still remained on the programme. Grandma, Jack, Aunt Mabel and Uncle Arthur.

Mrs Scarrot was a little concerned about Jack. As far as she knew he was still resting his voice but would he be able to resist the temptation to sing tonight? What else could he do if he didn't sing? On the other hand, what would the rest of the family do if he did? She smiled. They would put up with it, of course, and applaud. As Jenny had said, it was Christmas after all!

She was not worried about Aunt Mabel. Aunt Mabel had been on the stage; she was the only professional amongst them. But Uncle Arthur ... Well, they had all played guessing games in the past week about Uncle Arthur. What could a man do who wouldn't speak? Mime? Another tap dance? They would soon find out. But now it was time for Grandma, and Mrs Scarrot got up to go to the piano.

When Grandma walked on to the stage and stood beside the piano, one hand along its top and the other pressed to the front of her crimson flowered silk dress, the audience smiled. Of course, Grandma was going to sing, that was quite obvious. But after a few bewildered moments the audience came to the conclusion that Grandma must have switched off her hearing aid, for while Mrs Scarrot was playing 'You'll Never Walk Alone' from Carousel, Grandma was singing 'I Feel Pretty' from West Side Story.

Mrs Scarrot began to falter, then made a brave attempt to join in with Grandma's song, but without the music she was lost. She gave the audience an apologetic glance and rose to rummage through the contents of the piano stool. Grandma carried on, head flung back, eyes closed in blissful appreciation of her own performance, unaware that Mrs Scarrot had ceased playing, and equally unaware when Mrs Scarrot, unsuccessful in her search, returned to the piano and tried again.

Grandma made it even more difficult when she began to sing faster and faster. She had a strong voice for an elderly lady, perhaps because she practised talking so much, and the words of her romantic little song boomed out as if she was trying to make them heard all the way to Lands End. It was not long before Poppy began to giggle behind her handkerchief, Mr Scarrot's shoulders started to shake, Aunt Mabel gave a snort and Jenny chewed hard on her lip until it hurt. When Mrs Scarrot gave up and laid her head against the top of the piano, the audience collapsed altogether. But Grandma sang on, ignoring the bowed heads and shaking shoulders, and acknowledged the riotous applause at the end as if it was only to be expected.

When it was Jack's turn he slipped out of the room. As the curtains opened for his Act the family expected he would be wearing his satin suit, but instead he was seated, in his ordinary clothes, on a small chair at the centre of the stage. In his hands he held his guitar.

Within seconds he had his audience spellbound. For Jack, since his voice broke, had been practising and practising in the soundproof secrecy of the music room and now he showed his family that even if his voice had let him down, he could at least play the guitar. And it was not rock music that he played, but Christmas music, folk songs, lullabies and dances, one after the other. And finally he played a selection of Christmas carols, and as the last soft note of 'Away in a Manger' died away Mrs Scarrot wiped a tear from her eye.

'Oh Jack, that was beautiful. Beautiful.'

There were murmurs of agreement from everyone, and more than one handkerchief was sneaked back into a pocket. Then they applauded. They clapped and clapped and clapped until their hands were sore and Jack's face was red with embarrassment and pleasure, and when he left the stage he was hugged and patted on the back until he was even redder.

Aunt Mabel had been so affected by his performance that she had lost one of her eyelashes and there was some confusion until it was recovered. She took a long time to change, but when the curtains opened and the audience saw her in all her finery they decided she was well worth waiting for.

Aunt Mabel wore a long dress that swelled over her plump body and flowed out at the hem in a series of flounces. It was scarlet, and glittered in the lamplight. On top of her tower of golden hair she wore a plume of black feathers fastened with a comb of diamond-like stones, and around her neck was flung a long feather boa, trailing almost to the floor.

She swaggered to the front of the stage, a broad smile on her face, and in a big riproaring voice began to sing:

My old man said follow the van, and don't dilly dally on the way,

Orf went the van with me' ome packed in it,

Oi walked be'ind with me old cock linnet ...

'Come, on, everybody,' she shouted. 'Join in and sing with me!'

Delighted, the family obeyed and the children stamped their feet until the roof was almost lifted off.

After 'My Old Man' Aunt Mabel led them in a dozen old Music Hall songs, and where the children didn't know the words they hummed as the grown ups sang. By the time Aunt Mabel, still going strong, came to the end of the last verse the others had almost lost their voices.

'Now it's Uncle Arthur's turn,' she shouted. 'Go on, Arthur, go and get ready. You're the Grande Finale!'

There were whispers amongst the children as they waited. What was Uncle Arthur going to do? And what was a Grande Finale? Wasn't it supposed to be something special? But what could Uncle Arthur do that would be special? Jenny and Tommy were so busy whispering suggestions to each other that they almost missed the opening of the curtains, and it was Poppy's gasp that whipped their eyes back to the stage.

There was Uncle Arthur, seated in the small chair that Jack had used, and on his knee was a little figure with a round cheery face, a glowing red nose and bright eyes that rolled around as he surveyed the audience. The figure wore a black suit and a black cap, all covered with tiny pearl buttons, forming beautiful patterns of squares, diamonds and circles.

'Oh, isn't he lovely!' breathed Jenny.

'It's a ventriloquist's dummy,' whispered Jack. 'But how - how ... ?'

And then for the first time they heard Uncle Arthur's voice. It came, not from his own mouth but from the wide painted lips of the little wooden figure on his knee.

The eyes rolled, a small hand was raised in greeting and the lips opened.

'Hello, folks. Know who I am? I'm the Pearly King of Stratford!' He jerked a thumb sideways. 'Take no notice of *him,* it's me you should be watching!' He laughed and jiggled up and down on Uncle Arthur's knee, then tapped his cest. 'Well, me little bows an' arrows, 'ow d'you like the old whistle and flute, eh? There's more than a thousand buttons on me all afloat, and another thousand on me council 'ouses! What d'you think of that?'

The children stared at the little Pearly King in bewilderment. He jiggled up and down, shaking his head at their ignorance.

'You ain't understood one word I've said, 'ave you? Ain't you never 'eard of Cockney rhyming slang?' He stared at them with his fixed merry smile. The painted eyebrows above his bright eyes rose up and down.

'Whistle and flute? Suit! And a suit's made up of an 'all afloat' - coat, and 'council houses' - trousers.' He patted each in turn. 'See? It's easy when you think about it, ain't it?'

'Now then, nippers.' He leaned forward and peered at each child in turn. 'I'll tell you what I'm going to do. I'm going to tell you a story, all in rhyming slang, and you see if you can guess what it's all about.'

Jenny gave a little giggle of anticipation as the Pearly King settled back on Uncle Arthur's knees, crossed his legs and gave Aunt Mabel a big wink with his right eye.

'One day,' he said. 'Me and my trouble and strife ... ' He paused.

'Wife?' Poppy ventured.

'Clever girl!' beamed the Pearly King. 'Me and me trouble and strife went out for a ball o' chalk along the frog and toad '... '

'Walk?' suggested Jack.

'In the road!' shouted Tommy. 'In the road!'

'What bright nippers you all are,' said the Pearly King. 'Well, I'd got my best whistle and flute on ... '

'Suit!' yelled Jenny.

' ... and in me wallet I'd got all me bees and honey ... '

Bees and money? 'Oh, *money*!' said Poppy.

'Cos we were going to buy a new Cain and Abel, four new Vanity Fairs and a dickery dock!'

'Table!' shouted Jack.

'Chairs?' guessed Jenny.

'Dickery dock, dickery dock - CLOCK!' shrieked Tommy.

This was fun, the children decided and they leaned forward, hardly breathing, their eyes glued to the small cheery figure before them.

'Suddenly this Queens Park Ranger comes rushing up behind me ... '

Queens Park Ranger? No, that was too difficult.

'And hits me right in the north and south with his fist.'

'Mouth, mouth!'

'Well, I spat out two of my Hampstead Heath ... '

'TEETH!'

And then he hits me again on the Gungah Din!'

'Chin?'

'Would you Adam and Eve it?' asked the Pearly King.

'Believe it!' yelled Jenny. 'Believe it!'

'Well, I'm lying there looking up at a blue apple pie ('Sky?') with a big bruise on the back of my alive or dead ('Head!') and all of a sudden this la-di-dah drives up and stops beside me ('Car?' guessed Mrs Scarrot, joining in) and out jumps one of me old chinas who's struck it rich - china's short for china plate,' he explained.

'Mate,' returned Jack.

'He grabs this Queens Park Ranger, slips a pair of handcuffs on him and bundles 'im into the la-di-dah, just like that, while me trouble and strife has still got her hands over her mince pies, not knowing what's going on!'

'Oh, eyes!' realised Poppy.

'Turns out me old china's a copper now, Chief Inspector, no less, and in three weeks' time he's got that nasty little tealeaf ('Thief,' said Mrs Scarrot) up before a garden gate!'

'Er - magistrate?' guessed Mr Scarrot.

'Anyway, me old trouble and strife and me, we decided it was daft to carry all that bees and honey about, so we took it all to the J Arthur Rank ('Bank?' suggested Poppy) and got a cheque book instead!'

The Pearly King leaned back and with his hand covered a big yawn. 'And now it's almost midnight, so I'll sing you a little song before we finish.'

He sang his song but the children wouldn't let him go. They yelled for more and more, and the Pearly King gave them another little story, two jokes and a second short song, before they allowed him to leave the stage.

The audience had become oblivious to Uncle Arthur's part in the performance and it was not until he stood up and bowed, the little Pearly King now hanging limp and lifeless from his hand, that they remembered and realised it had been Uncle Arthur all the time.

'Oh, Uncle Arthur, that was marvellous!' said Poppy. 'How ever did you do it?'

But Uncle Arthur gave her his usual silent smile, and to all the admiring comments and eager questions he answered with that same silent but happy smile, until at last the family realised that he would not speak and that they would have to wait to hear his voice again until some far off day when the little Pearly King was brought out once more from his hiding place.

19

Endings and Beginnings

Christmas Day was over. Outside in the dark quiet night more snow began to fall, deepening the white blanket that lay over the island and drifting against the doors and windows of the Scarrots' house. Inside a slow smoky spiral still rose from the dying embers of the sitting room fire but all else was still and silent.

It had been a long day, full of pleasure and excitement, bringing a deep contented sleep to some, while those who dreamed saw only happiness in their visions.

Jenny dreamed. She dreamed she was drifting down the Grand Canal of Venice in a magnificent swan-shaped gondola, while beside her Mr Tulley of Stellar Travel Limited, in a black suit decorated with pearl buttons, signed a never-ending succession of tickets and vouchers which he placed in eleven neat piles.

Tommy dreamed as he lay in his warm blankets with Cadbury smuggled out of the basket in the hall and into his bed. He dreamed that he and the little brown kitten were seated at the kitchen table before plates of turkey sandwiches, mixed pickles and chocolate truffles, and in his sleep his lips curved.

Sleep was very close to Poppy, but just before her eyes closed she made up her mind that she was going to be a singer, and her last waking vision was of herself in a long white dress singing to a rapt audience at the Royal Albert Hall, London.

Jack was asleep, as were Charlie, Grampa and Grandma. Aunt

Mabel, having said goodnight to Uncle Arthur and waited for his silent answering squeeze of her shoulder, turned on her side and pulled the sheet up to the tips of her round plump ears.

In the end bedroom of the house, the one that faced over the lake towards Colonel Fitzbudgett's mansion, Mr Scarrot was asleep. Mrs Scarrot lay beside him, staring out of the little window at the luminous Christmas sky.

So many nice things had happened in the year that was coming to a close. It had been a good year. And there were good things to look forward to in the year to come. The holiday in Venice. And later ...

She smiled and snuggled down under the bedclothes. No one else knew yet. She would tell Mr Scarrot on New Year's Eve, she had decided, and then they would tell the children. She closed her eyes and began her favourite going-to-sleep occupation. She had reached the aitches now: Hugh, Horace, Humphrey? Hilary? But wasn't that a girl's name? It was going to be a boy, she was sure. Harold? Harry? Perhaps. Harry Scarrot. Fred would like that, it was his grandfather's name.

A sudden thought struck Mrs Scarrot and she smiled. Perhaps she wouldn't wait for New Year's Eve after all. Perhaps she'd tell him now.

She leaned over and shook her husband's shoulder.

'Fred? Fred, wake up!'

'Wha - Whassa - '

'I've got something to tell you.'

What?' Mr Scarrot, awake now, propped himself on one elbow and stared at his wife.

A crafty gleam had entered her eye. 'I'll tell you a secret if you tell me one.'

'Go on, then.'

'No, you first,' said Mrs Scarrot. 'Tell me, Fred ... What *was* it you did for the Colonel? What was it *really*?'

THE END

AN EXTRACT FROM 'THE MYSTERY OF CRAVEN MANOR'

Then he took a deep breath and began to climb.

He had not been prepared for all the soot. He had expected to get dirty but he could never have imagined the thick choking blanket that began to smother him as he climbed. Every movement he made brought more soot cascading down, silting up his eyes and nose and mouth until he felt he was being buried alive. He couldn't breathe.

Panic filled him, but he managed to turn his face downwards and draw a single vile-tasting breath. Then he willed himself to remain motionless, eyes and lips tightly closed, lungs bursting, until the soot gradually settled.

Cautiously he took another deep breath, held it, and climbed another few inches, fingers and feet groping for crevices. The soot swirled again and he waited again, then moved upwards a little further. It was tiring work and panic kept threatening to overwhelm him but he was winning, he told himself. The constant pauses made progress slow but he thought he must be halfway by now, perhaps on a level with the ceiling of his bedroom. There was still the shaft that went up through the top floor of the house, the attic floor, but after that he would be within a few feet of the opening.

And then he slipped. The notch into which he had wedged his right foot suddenly crumbled, his fingers lost their grip and he was plunging down through the blackness, chin, wrists, elbows and knees painfully scraping against the old stones. He didn't fall all the way to the bottom. His fall ended with a few final agonising scrapes and he found himself wedged, still upright but with one knee jammed against his stomach and his left sleeve caught on some small projection above his head. The soot swirled in a dense cloud and the inside of his mouth was caked with the stuff. His lungs were empty, the air knocked out of them by his fall, and panic-stricken he wanted to snatch mouthfuls of the thick black atmosphere around him, like a drowning man gulps water. But somehow he forced himself to wait until the soot settled.

Printed in Great Britain
by Amazon

38854872R00067